A Barr Colony Adventure

Full Steam
to CANADA

To my grandchildren:
Jadyn Lydia, Ada Marie,
Callista Rose and Seamus Patrick,
who will find their names in this story.
Jasper Alexander, who wasn't born
at the time of writing, will find a
single mention of his name,
with more to come in the next book.

Table of Contents

1

Autumn, 1902

Millions of Acres

D orothy Bolton plunked down hard on the chair. It wasn't fair. After a boring day at school, she had to do more tedious drills at night. With a loud sigh, she started copying a page of sums into her practice book.

Dorothy didn't mind that she was behind in arithmetic. It wasn't her fault she'd had the typhoid fever last spring and missed three months of school. Unfortunately, her teacher cared. This term Miss Davis lent Mam a textbook so Dorothy could catch up.

She glanced around from the kitchen table. Beside the fireplace, her big brother, Frank, was teasing his frisky terrier. That wasn't fair either. He could play with Chap while she had to sit still and do computations. And he could relax near the glowing coals, while she shivered under a shawl.

Dorothy pictured herself walking to the hearth and tossing the thin brown text into the fire. She imagined the flick of her wrist as she flung the nuisance away.

"Stop dawdling, Dodie. Sooner started, sooner done." Her mother's voice jolted Dorothy from her daydream just as *Practical Arithmetic* exploded in flames.

"Yes, Mam." Dorothy squirmed in her seat. She couldn't even look sideways without her mother noticing.

"And sit up straight. Your back will be permanently curved if you carry on slouching." Mam's knitting needles clicked while her rocker creaked.

With a huff, Dorothy straightened her back.

From the parlour she heard her older sister plodding through scales on the piano. Since Lydia started lessons last summer, she had practised the same exercises every night. The noise rattled Dorothy's brain. No wonder she couldn't keep her mind on arithmetic.

Dorothy wished they could send the bloomin' piano back to Gram, but Gram didn't have space since she moved in with Uncle Oliver.

Dorothy had finished half of tonight's assignment when her father burst in the kitchen door. The damp autumn air rushed in with him. Looking up, Dorothy tugged her blue woolen shawl tighter.

"Gather round, family," announced Dad, waving a folded newspaper. He dragged the carver's chair to the table, grating it across the stone floor. Dorothy flinched. Mam made everyone lift the chairs, but Dad always forgot when he was excited.

Under his generous bristly moustache, Dad's mouth stretched in a grin. Dorothy smiled back. Whatever he had in mind was bound to be more interesting than arithmetic. She stuck the well-chewed pencil into her frizzy hair.

Lydia came from the parlour and sat, hands folded primly on her lap. Frank carried his chair to the table.

Mam's fingers kept knitting. In the expectant silence, everyone stared at the tall, lean man.

Dad's usually tired face glowed. "Down at The Red Lion, there was this man fresh from Canada —"

"Were you drinking at the pub again?" interrupted Mam.

"Only 'alf a pint, cross me 'eart." Dad reached over to pat Mam's shoulder. "You know I'm a family man, luv."

"Go on, Dad," encouraged Frank. "The man from Canada…"

"Well, he's here briefly visiting his folks. He got himself a homestead in the North-West Territories. Said the Canadian Government is giving away millions of acres of farmland."

Mam sniffed. "He spun a story and had the whole pub spellbound, no doubt."

Dad looked a little sheepish. "Well, quite a few of us was interested."

Dorothy's head spun with questions. Did she dare interrupt? She rubbed her finger over a dent in the old oak table.

"Don't believe none what you hear," said Mam, "and only half what you see."

"Ha! I knew you'd say that, Aggie, so I brought something to see." Dad spread the newspaper on the table. "Even the *Manchester Guardian* says so." He pointed to the headline on page five: "Free Land in Canada."

"Where's Canada?" asked Dorothy.

Nobody answered.

Frank leaned close to read the article. "Listen to this: 'Elk and deer abound on the prairies. All a man needs is a sharp eye and a steady hand to shoot game for his family year round'."

"How is that possible?" asked Mam. "What about the gamekeepers?"

"That's the point, luv. There ain't no gamekeepers. Not like 'ere where all the land is owned by rich folk that won't share a single rabbit with a starvin' family." Dad talked so fast, he had to stop for breath.

Dorothy blurted out, "No gamekeepers, Dad?"

"That's right, my pet."

"That's good! Ada's dad went to jail for catching just ONE FISH!" Dorothy remembered her best friend crying at this very table as she told the story. Dorothy hated the gamekeeper who had reported Ada's father for poaching.

Frank still had his nose in the newspaper. "By golly, you can register for free land in the North-West when you're eighteen years old. I'm seventeen and a half right now." Frank's brown eyes gleamed and his face started glowing like Dad's.

Mam stood, still holding the knitting. Her eyes narrowed and her mouth tightened into a thin line. Her creamy skin flushed pink.

Oh, no, thought Dorothy, *please, don't have another row.* Her stomach bunched into knots whenever her parents argued.

"Shame on you, William," Mam sputtered. "Putting such notions in our son's head. He's too young to go to some wilderness halfway round the world by himself."

"Of course he is, Aggie," soothed Dad. "We're all going with him."

Mam's knitting dropped from her hand.

4

Lydia nudged Dorothy, gesturing at the floor. Dorothy returned a dagger look. Lydia poked harder. Scowling, Dorothy knelt to pick up the knitting.

"Here, Mam."

Drawing a deep breath, Mam sat again. "Our girls will not go to the North-West Territories. It's no place for proper young ladies like Lydia. And Dorothy has not finished her book learning. She cannot go to a wilderness where there are no schools."

No proper young ladies! No schools! Dorothy stared at Dad.

"You know 'ow I want me own farm, Aggie," Dad said wistfully. "The paper says to act now or the best land will be taken." Dad's moustache jiggled as he kneaded his lips. "But you've made a point. The North-West would not be suitable for our girls."

Mam cleared her throat. "I know you dislike your desk job, Willy –"

Dad interrupted, "Aye, I'm weary of warming the seat of a stool."

Dorothy sympathized. She was weary of her desk at school, too.

"Nevertheless," Mam continued, "work was never meant to be enjoyed. It brings home a living. And Frank has been with Marley's Imports for two years. He's still a junior clerk, but he works hard and he'll move up in the company."

Frank's eyebrows jumped at the unexpected compliment. Dorothy smiled at him but he didn't notice. He was reading the newspaper article again.

"As you wish, Aggie," Dad said finally. "We're getting

on well enough here."

Mam nodded with a slight smile. Gathering her skirt, she swept from the room.

After Mam left, Dorothy burst out, "Where's Canada, Dad? What's a wilderness? Is it true there are no schools?"

"Haven't you learned anything?" asked Lydia, flicking a crumb off the table. "I know all about the Canadian wilderness. Nothing but rough men and wild animals. I certainly don't intend to go there." Imitating Mam's dignity, she minced back to the parlour.

Dorothy got up to close the door. She peered through the etched-glass pane as Lydia settled herself at the piano bench. *You're so prissy*, thought Dorothy.

In a minute, "Flow Gently, Sweet Afton" spurted into the kitchen, one halting phrase at a time. Dorothy gritted her teeth; Lydia had been practising that song all week. Through the piano noise Dorothy heard Dad's voice: "You sound interested, Dodie."

Dorothy wrapped her arms around Dad's shoulders, rubbing her cheek against his short wiry curls. "I'll go anywhere with you, Daddy," she promised. "Especially anywhere that doesn't have schools."

Dad took the newspaper back from Frank and whispered, "I'll find out more about it. Best not tell your mother yet. We don't want to get her riled up without reason."

Several weeks passed without another word about Canada. Finally Dorothy asked, "Dad, are you still thinking about Cana...?" He put his finger to his lips. He hadn't forgotten! It wouldn't do to press him; he would say something when he was ready.

The next day Dorothy walked home from church with Ada. Every Saturday night Ada's mother wrapped her hair in rags. Dorothy marvelled at the silky brown ringlets cascading under Ada's bonnet. Mam always said it was useless to fuss with Dorothy's unruly mop and just tied it back with a bow.

Dorothy took Ada's hand. They were both wearing their Sunday gloves. Dorothy's ivory silk gloves with pearl buttons were a present from Gram. Ada's white cotton gloves had been mended with tiny stitches.

"I have a secret," whispered Dorothy. Then she hesitated. Was she breaking Dad's confidence? No, he had cautioned her not to talk to Mam. She could tell her best friend. "My dad's thinking about going to Canada."

Ada stared at Dorothy. "Oh Dodie! So far away?"

Dorothy nodded. "Do you know where it is?"

Ada squeezed her eyebrows together. "It's somewhere across the ocean. When Dad's cousin went there, it took months for a letter to get back to us." Ada's eyes lit up. "Why not ask Miss Davis tomorrow?"

At morning break, Dorothy and Ada lingered in the cloakroom behind their class. "Go on," whispered Ada, pushing Dorothy into the classroom. "I'll wait for you."

Miss Davis sat at her desk marking the penmanship exercise the class had just completed. Shuffling her feet, Dorothy looked resentfully at the stack of papers. After precisely copying each letter until her fingers ached, she had better get a good grade.

Finally Miss Davis looked up. "Yes, Dorothy?"

Dorothy swallowed. "May I trouble you, uh, to tell

me where Canada is?"

Miss Davis removed her reading spectacles. "What has brought on this sudden interest in Canada?"

"Well, uh...my...my dad's cousin went there," stammered Dorothy, feeling a little guilty for the lie.

As Miss Davis pulled down the world map, she explained, "Great Britain has many colonies." Using her wooden pointer, she indicated Australia, India, South Africa and other smaller countries. They were all coloured the same shade of pink. "And here's our biggest colony, Canada."

Dorothy stared at the map. Canada was a huge mass of pink, far larger than the little island where she lived. How could one country be that big?

"We shall study the Empire later this year. Do you have any more questions now, Dorothy?"

"Where are the North-West Territories?"

Miss Davis looked at her oddly. "Is your family planning to emigrate?"

"What does that mean?"

"It means 'move to a different country'."

Dorothy hesitated at the need for another lie. "No, nothing like that. Uh...thank you, Miss Davis." Dorothy scooted to the cloakroom, grabbed her coat and ran down the hall with Ada.

2

Winter, 1903

Not an Easy Decision

Dorothy sat at the oak table with her arithmetic book open, dreaming about the vast pink country of Canada. Where was the land that Dad wanted?

In the rocking chair near the fireplace, Mam was knitting. "It feels bitter cold tonight, Willy. Would you add more coal to the fire?"

Dad walked to the hearth and poured another scuttleful of coal over the grate. "What a price they charge for coal these days," he complained. After a minute he added, "You can get wood for free in Canada."

Mam's needles clicked furiously. "Mercy, William, are you still on about Canada?"

Hunching her shoulders, Dorothy held the textbook up like a shield. She heard Dad scrape his chair close to Mam.

"I read a letter in the *Manchester Guardian* about the North-West," he said excitedly. "It was written by Reverend I. M. Barr."

Dorothy peeked over her book.

"I sent for more information and I got this from Mr. Barr's office." Dad pulled a thick pamphlet from his pocket. "We can get one hundred sixty acres *each* for me and Frank. Imagine – our own farm spreading farther than the eye can see in all directions!"

Dad riffled through the pamphlet. "See how Mr. Barr describes the land: *'good climate, conducive to vigorous health…fertile soil…an abundant rainfall, with good water everywhere…excellent hay and pasturage'*."

Mam stopped knitting and stared at Dad with tight-pressed lips. Hardly daring to breathe, Dorothy looked from one parent to the other. Finally Mam said, "How can there be so much wonderful land that nobody owns? It sounds too good to be true."

Dad's words tumbled out. "It *is* true, luv. Mr. Barr is a man of the cloth. I'm sure 'e wouldn't lie. 'e's in Canada now, working with the government to pick the best 'omesteads for a big colony of Britishers."

Dorothy noticed Dad had slipped into the Yorkshire accent of his childhood, like he always did when he got excited. She knew what Mam would say next.

"Slow down, Willy," Mam directed. "You're dropping your h's again."

With pointed finger, Dad searched for a line of text. "Look, he wishes to keep the land *'in the hands of people of British birth.'* There'll be no foreigners near us."

Mam sighed. "I see you shan't rest until I consider it." She took the pamphlet and stuffed it into her knitting bag.

Pinning her eyes on Mam, Dorothy willed her to agree. *Yes, yes, yes! I want to work with Dad on our own farm.*

Several evenings later, the family sat around the table sipping their after-dinner tea. Mam took the steaming kettle from the hob and refilled the teapot. Then she handed the pamphlet back to Dad.

"The settlement does sound well organized, Willy, but I don't see why our family should go. Frank is settled in business, Lydia's getting on with her piano and…" Mam's voice got a slight quiver, "there's George to consider too."

Dorothy gasped. Not for one minute had she thought about George. Frank and Dad looked at each other sheepishly. They hadn't considered George either, and they had known him.

Lydia clinked her teacup into its saucer. "That's right, Mam. You and I visit George's grave every Sunday. Who will remember him if we leave?"

There was no retort to that argument and the talk about Canada stopped. It might have ended forever if Frank hadn't thumped into the house two weeks later. Dorothy was laying the table while Lydia baked scones. Mam was out delivering soup to an ill neighbour.

Without taking off his boots, Frank stomped upstairs and whistled for Chap to follow. A door slammed overhead, making the gaslights flicker. Dorothy stared at the ceiling. Frank had just broken three ironclad household rules.

She tiptoed upstairs and reached out to knock on his door. A muffled sound stopped her hand in mid-air. Peering through the keyhole, she watched Frank's arm pound the bed. His other arm hugged Chap while the dog's tail wagged furiously.

Finally she called, "Are you all right, Frank?"

"Go away, Dodie!"

With her hand to her mouth, Dorothy retreated downstairs.

When Mam and Dad arrived, Frank would not come down to eat. After dinner, Mam took a bowl of soup to his bedroom. Then she poured a fresh pot of tea and called Dad back to the table.

Dorothy walked back and forth carrying dirty dishes to the scullery. She strained to listen. "Frank lost his job," Mam said. "Mr. Marley's nephew returned from the Boer War and needed a position."

"Bloody rotten," said Dad. "He shan't get another job with all the veterans swarming back. Mr. Barr described this exact problem."

Dorothy's heart fluttered as she collected an armful of plates.

Closing her eyes, Mam sighed and rubbed her forehead. Then she took a deep breath. "No use crying over spilt milk," she said briskly. "Let me see that pamphlet again." Mam and Dad carried their tea to the parlour and shut the door.

Dorothy stacked the plates beside the scullery sink where Lydia was washing up. She grabbed Lydia's arm. "Our Frank lost his job. Mam is reading the pamphlet again. Maybe we'll go to the North-West Territories now!"

Lydia swung around. Her green eyes glinted dangerously. "The North-West Territories? Do you know what that means?"

"Yes," Dorothy gloated, "no school!"

"There's *nothing* there, Dodo. It's a wretched place!" Lydia flung a dishrag at her and fled upstairs.

Dorothy's heart thumped. *What does Lydia mean, 'nothing there'? She must be wrong. Dad wouldn't take us to a wretched place.*

Her heart settled again. With a sigh, she picked up the dishrag and sank her arms into the soapy water. She was scrubbing the soup pot when the parlour door clicked open. Setting the pot on a shelf, she hurried into the kitchen.

Mam had disappeared upstairs. Dad slouched in the carver's chair. Tiptoeing over, Dorothy whispered, "Shall we go to Canada now?"

"Possibly, my pet, but there's much thinking to do." Dad patted her hair. "The passage is very dear." Dad looked too tired for any more questions.

After school the next day, Dorothy and Ada buttoned their overcoats outside the girls' entrance. Ada's older brother, Tony, darted from behind a massive oak tree and snatched Dorothy's muffler. Waving it like a long red flag, he dared Dorothy to grab it.

Both girls chased him along Bootle Street, past the row of small shops that had been there for two hundred years. Dark clouds rolled overhead and a biting wind blew at their backs. In front of Burney's Butcher Shop, Tony hooted and dropped the muffler.

"Your brother's a beastly pest," said Dorothy, stooping to pick it up. She wrapped the muffler around her neck and thought of her own dear brother. "Our Frank lost his job."

"Oh, Dodie, what rotten luck," said Ada. "Now he'll take to drink like my dad."

Dorothy shuddered at the thought of Frank staggering home drunk every night. Shaking that nightmare from her mind, she reached for Ada's hand. "Mam might let us go to Canada instead."

For an instant the sun squeezed through the clouds, lighting up the street. A large globe gleamed in the window of The Olde Bookshoppe next door. Dorothy recognized the wide pink shape of Canada; suddenly she felt certain they would go.

She tugged Ada forward. "Come along, I have something to show you."

Panting, the two girls raced up the tree-lined path to the top of Stonegate Hill. They reached Old Newton Street leading to the row houses where Ada lived, but Dorothy pulled her the opposite way.

Ada giggled. "Are we going to church on Thursday?"

"Yes," said Dorothy.

When they reached St. Peter's Parish Church, Dorothy's eyes swept the cobblestone street. Horses clopped by pulling carriages, but nobody was standing nearby. She said, "I have to show you something in the graveyard."

Yanking her hand loose, Ada stared at Dorothy. "Are you daft? It's almost dusk. I don't want to go in there."

"It's important." Dorothy strode down the lane toward the walled-in churchyard.

Ada sprinted to catch up. "Very well. But let's not stay long."

When Dorothy tapped the wrought-iron gate, it creaked opened. Tangled vines covered the high stone walls. In a flash of sun, the leafless vines twisted like a mass of squirming snakes. Dorothy froze and Ada bumped into her.

"It's bloomin' spooky," whispered Ada. "Are you sure you want to go in?"

The sun disappeared again. The vines looked lifeless in the flat grey light. Dorothy stepped forward. A sudden gust of wind rattled the twisted branches. Her throat went dry. She swallowed hard.

"I haven't been here for a long time, but I'm certain I can find it."

"What are you looking for?" Ada asked in a tiny voice.

"A little gravestone with a baby angel carved on top."

"Dodie," Ada said doubtfully, "there are many baby gravestones here."

"It's near that corner."

Pulling Ada along, Dorothy tiptoed around pitted, moss-covered tombstones. She shivered, thinking how long those people had been buried. She hurried past small stones marking children's graves, trying not to think about them at all.

In the far corner stood new, smooth gravestones. Dorothy ignored the elaborate memorials surrounded by wrought-iron fences. She walked past humble markers of poured concrete and looked around uncertainly. Then she spied a small granite angel.

"There it is!"

Hurrying over, she knelt to feel the chiselled letters: *George Andrew Bolton: 2 years, 3 months*. She looked up at Ada. "My brother."

"Oh, Dodie, I'm sorry," gasped Ada. "I didn't know you had another brother."

"He died when I was five months old, so I don't

remember him. Mam and Lydia stop here every Sunday." Dorothy cleared her throat. "Mam is worried about George. He'll be lonely when we leave. Will you visit him sometimes?"

"Of course I shall. I'll ask Mother to stop with me after church." Ada pulled Dorothy up and hugged her. "Um… may we leave now?"

Holding hands, they ran all the way to Ada's back door. "Dodie," Ada said shyly, "I'll be lonely when you leave too." Ada dashed inside and Dorothy stood alone in the lane. She trudged home with a lump in her throat.

When she reached the back porch, Lydia wrenched open the door. Her green eyes narrowed into icy slits. "Wherever have you been?" she snapped as Dorothy hung her coat on its peg. "I've had to make dinner all alone."

"Where's Mam?"

"In the parlour with Dad and Frank."

Lydia's face was darker than the clouds outside. She slammed the breadboard on the table so hard, the loaf of bread bounced. Dorothy gaped as Lydia sawed the loaf into uneven chunks. She expected to see a finger fly off any minute.

"What are you staring at, Dodo?" fumed Lydia. She stabbed her breadknife toward the parlour door. "Tell them dinner is ready."

Dorothy hesitated. "Should I interrupt them?"

"Yes!" hissed Lydia. "I'm hungry."

Dorothy peeked through the glass pane. Mam and Frank sat on the brocade sofa. Mam looked serious, but not angry. Frank was… she looked again. Was that a smile? Dorothy knocked and Dad waved from the mahogany parlour chair.

When they stood, Dorothy noticed that Frank had grown even taller than Dad. She looked up as he walked through the doorway. "I'm sorry you lost your job, Frank."

Frank patted her hair. "Don't fret, Dodie-Podie. I'm over it now."

After everyone sat, Lydia ladled chunky stew into their bowls. Mam cleared her throat and announced, "Dad and I have decided that the best future for our family lies with the Barr Colony in the North-West Territories." She sighed heavily. "This was not an easy decision."

Dad would get his farm! Dorothy looked at him and felt a grin starting.

Lydia dropped the ladle, spattering gravy and potato chunks over Dorothy's school pinafore. Dorothy jumped. "Take care, you clumsy –"

Mam frowned. "Be quiet, Dodie. Least said, soonest mended."

Dorothy glowered at Lydia. *What miserable company you'll be in Canada*, she thought.

3

Spring, 1903
No Useless Articles

orothy sat on her bed cradling a life-sized baby doll. She hugged its soft body and stroked the smooth porcelain hands. Holding it up, she watched blue eyes open on the delicately painted face. Its gown and bonnet were the exact same shade of blue.

Dorothy had seen the doll in the window of Mrs. Bedwin's Toy Emporium. During Sunday dinner she told Gram how beautiful it was. At the time, Lydia had scoffed, "You're too old for dolls."

Later, Dorothy and Gram walked downtown and stared through the store window. Gram commented, "That's not a child's toy. That doll needs an older girl who will value it." When Dorothy confided she would name the doll George, Gram squeezed her hand.

Gram gave her the doll for her tenth birthday in February. "It's my last chance to spoil my grand-daughter," Gram said when Mam questioned the extravagant present.

Wrapping the doll in a blanket, Dorothy laid it in the steamer trunk she and Lydia were sharing.

"You can't bring that!" Lydia yanked out the bundle and held it above her head.

Dorothy jumped to snatch at it. "Put it back, you beast," she shouted. "It's my favourite thing."

Mam stood at their bedroom door. "Girls, stop your row," she said wearily.

"Mam, she can't take a doll. Mr. Barr's letter said no useless articles."

"That's not a useless article," cried Dorothy. "That's George!"

The room fell silent as Mam and Lydia stared. Dorothy gulped. She hadn't told the doll's secret name to anyone except Gram.

"Put George in the trunk." Mam's voice was soft as the breeze ruffling the new spring leaves outside.

"Thanks, Mam." Dorothy hugged her mother, flashing a smug smile at Lydia.

Dorothy knew many favourite things had been sold or given away. Gram had agreed to sell the piano to help pay their passage. After the carters removed it, Lydia sat in the parlour a long time staring at the empty space.

Yesterday Frank and Dorothy took Chap to Uncle Oliver's cottage. Uncle Oliver worked a small acreage at the edge of town. "Chap will be happy," Frank said as they left. "He'll have much more room to run."

Dorothy remembered looking back at the ivy-covered cottage. Chap hadn't looked happy. He barked frantically with his nose pressed against the garden gate. Frank hadn't looked happy either. He kept his head down, kicking stones along the path.

Mam's voice brought Dorothy back to the present, "...that party frock has no use in the wilderness." Mam pointed to the green velveteen dress draped over the steamer lid.

Dorothy stared at her favourite dress. "But, Mam," she pleaded, "at the Christmas pageant Ada said that dress made my hair glow like copper."

"Practical clothes only, Dodie. You'll outgrow that fancy frock long before you have any opportunity to wear it."

Then Dorothy remembered the farm. "Oh well, I won't need it out in the fields."

"In the fields!" scoffed Mam. "Won't you ever start thinking like a lady? You'll be helping me in the house." Then her voice lightened. "That dress would look becoming on Ada too. Why don't you take it to her?"

By afternoon, Dorothy had a canvas bag stuffed with clothes unsuitable for the wilderness. She ran round the block and down the back lane to Ada's house.

"Oh, Dodie," said Ada, "I thought you'd be too busy to come. I planned to stop by your house tonight."

"I brought you some things that are too fancy to take."

Ada's brother, Tony, was polishing his boots beside the hearth. "Jolly good thinking," he mocked. "Fancy clothes won't help you fight off the bears."

Dorothy stared at him. "What are you on about, Tony?"

"They're everywhere in the wilderness," taunted Tony. He knocked off Dorothy's straw hat and grabbed her thick hair. "They'll bite your head off for dinner." He cuffed her head with his hand.

"That's not true!" yelled Dorothy, twisting out of his grasp. "Dad wouldn't take us to a dangerous place."

Ada kicked his shin. "Get outta here, or I'll tell Mother you were rude to my guest." Grabbing his boots, Tony slammed out the back door.

"Take no mind of him," said Ada. "He just wishes he were going too." She opened the cutlery drawer in the kitchen table. "I hid something for you. Tony would never look here because he never lays the table."

Pulling out an envelope, Ada said proudly, "I got this at the stationery shop in exchange for sweeping."

Dorothy read Ada's name and address penned in neat handwriting on the envelope. Inside she found two pieces of linen writing paper.

"Miss Davis helped me get the address right," said Ada. She grabbed Dorothy's hand. "I shall miss you so much, Dodie. Please write to me."

Dorothy tried to answer but a giant lump filled her throat. "Thank you, Ada," she choked out. "I *will* write. Uh, I ought to go now."

Halfway down the lane, she turned to look back. Ada still stood outside her door, waving slowly. "You're my best friend," Dorothy called. "I'll never forget you." As she ran home, her heart ached. She already missed Ada dreadfully.

Back home the kitchen was in a jumble. Stacks of crockery, pans and linen filled the table. Lydia tucked a box into the large wooden crate marked *Wm. Bolton, c/o Rev. I. M. Barr, British Colony, Saskatoon, District of Saskatchewan, Canada.*

Dorothy read the label on the box: Price's Paraffin Candles. "Why do we need all those candles?"

"There won't be gaslights on the wall," Lydia said

impatiently. "We're going to the wilderness, remember, Dodo?"

Dorothy stuck out her tongue. Then Dad walked in with a bundle of striped cloth. "What's that, Dad?" she asked.

Dad dropped the pile on the floor. There were five sections doubled over and sewn. "Our mattresses," he said excitedly.

Dorothy felt the rough cotton ticking. "But they're so flat!"

"We'll stuff them with straw when we need them."

Dorothy's hand flew to her mouth as she stared at the limp cotton sheets.

Dad ruffled her hair. "Don't worry, my lamb. They'll be comfortable."

"We had tea, Dodie," said Lydia. "There's something in the pantry for you."

On the middle shelf, Dorothy found two pieces of buttered bread. The rest of the shelves were bare. The everyday stoneware dishes with the blue cornflowers were gone. The tins of flour, sugar and tea were gone. The linen tablecloth and napkins for special meals were gone too.

As she ate, Dorothy stared at the empty shelves. Her familiar world had been erased, just like the blackboards got wiped clean at school. Then she noticed the very top shelf was still full.

In the kitchen, Mam was wrapping the stoneware dishes in newspaper.

"Aren't we taking the fancy dishes, Mam?"

"No, Dodie, bone china is too fragile. I'm giving

them to Aunt Catherine. She and Uncle Charley are coming to clean out the house after we leave."

Dorothy sighed. She loved the delicate dishes with misty blue castles painted on white porcelain. Another piece of her life swept away!

Frank's voice jolted through Dorothy's thoughts. "Did you buy a gun, Dad?"

Dad laughed. "Frank, neither of us has any idea how to fire a gun."

Frank frowned. "Mr. Barr said to bring one." He grabbed Reverend Barr's Christmas letter from the mantel. It was ragged from repeated readings.

Frank riffled through the pages. "Aha!" He read aloud: *"If you possess a sewing machine, take it, also a gun, if you have one."*

Mam looked up from her packing. "We do possess a sewing machine so we're taking it. We don't own a gun so we're not taking one. I don't want my son shot to pieces before he gets proper instruction in the use of firearms."

Frank's shoulders sagged until Dad playfully cuffed him on the back. "There are veterans joining our colony. We'll buy a gun in Saskatoon and ask them to teach us."

That night Dorothy was sent to bed while the others continued cramming final articles into crates, trunks and leather bags. She slept fitfully between dreams of bears biting off her head and Frank shooting himself full of holes.

At dawn she awoke with her stomach in knots. Did Dad really know what he was doing, taking the family so far away from England?

4

March 30 & 31, 1903
Fairly on the Briny

Clattering and clomping sounds startled Dorothy awake. Then a voice yelled, *"Bloody 'ell, Lydia, keep that 'orse still!"*

Dorothy scrambled to the window and pushed it open. There were no lace curtains to block her view. Leaning out, she peered down to the street.

Uncle Oliver's hay wagon was there. Lydia stood beside old Tom, pulling the reins tight and patting his nose. Dad, Frank and Uncle Oliver grunted under the weight of a large crate and finally heaved it onto the wagon.

Dorothy heard Mam's voice fretting, "Be careful."

"Hi, Uncle Oliver," Dorothy called.

Uncle Oliver looked up and laughed. "What in blazes are you doing, girlie? You'll fall on your head if you lean any further out."

"Close the window, Dodie," said Mam. "Get dressed and bring your sheets and eiderdown to the kitchen." Mam's face looked pinched and tired. *Follow instructions immediately*, Dorothy told herself.

Dorothy yanked off her flannel nightgown. Shivering, she pulled on her petticoat and the blue serge dress Mam had laid out. She stuffed the nightgown into her leather travel bag and ran downstairs, dragging her bedclothes behind her.

Mam set bread, cheese and rashers on the table. The fancy cups and saucers sat beside the pot of tea. Dorothy blinked. *For breakfast?*

After eating, the family rushed back outside. "Clean up, Dodie," Mam called over her shoulder. "We can't leave dirty dishes for Aunt Catherine."

As she washed the delicate cups and saucers, an idea formed in Dorothy's mind. Her feather quilt and flannel sheets weren't packed yet.

Soon Lydia and Frank came for the last trunk. "Where is your bedding, Dodie?" asked Lydia.

Dorothy pointed to the bumpy material at the top of the trunk. "In there."

Lydia looked surprised. "Good girl," she said, snapping the lid closed.

Dorothy followed them out with her leather bag. Dad tossed it into the wagon and flashed a rueful smile. "This is it, family."

They all stared at the cozy brick house until Uncle Oliver checked his pocket watch. "Shake a leg, folks, or you'll miss the train!"

Uncle Oliver helped Mam onto the wagon seat and the others climbed into the back. With a word from Uncle Oliver, old Tom trotted forward. Perched atop a crate, Dorothy clung to Frank as they bounced along the cobblestone street. She watched her house grow smaller until they turned a corner.

Already Dorothy missed her home. Then she remembered Dad's promise. In Canada they wouldn't have to rent. They would build their own house and own it.

When the wagon clopped up to the train station, several young men cheered. "My mates from the office," said Frank, jumping down. They thumped him on the back and wished him well.

The young men moved the baggage off the wagon into the stationmaster's care. Just in time! A train whistle tooted sharply down the track, then a massive steam engine huffed to a stop like a tired black beast. Dorothy's feet danced; she had never ridden a train before.

One of the youths pressed a slim book into Lydia's hand. Lydia blushed, looking shyly at the ground. Dorothy froze in mid-step. Did Lydia have a sweetheart?

Mam steered Lydia and Dorothy toward the family. Aunt Catherine held her arms out and a moan escaped from Mam's throat. "Oh, sister, I shan't ever see you again."

Aunt Catherine smiled crookedly. "Certain, you will. You'll be back for a visit soon." Dorothy could see Aunt Catherine didn't believe that.

Gram opened a large string bag. "I have farewell presents for my three darlings."

She handed Frank a narrow red velvet case. He looked inside and whistled. "Gram! One of the new Lucky Curve fountain pens."

"There's enough ink for the sea journey. You can buy ink to refill it in Canada." Gram pulled a leather-bound book from her bag. "Keep a careful diary, boy."

Gram kissed Lydia on the cheek, thrusting a songbook into her hands. "There will be another piano in Canada, my beauty. Make people happy by playing for them."

Dorothy stared at her grandmother, trying to fix Gram's image in her mind: her soft blue eyes, the happy crinkles in her cheeks when she smiled.

Gram cleared her throat. "Agatha and William, you made this decision for the best welfare of your family. Go with our blessing."

"Gram!" cried Dorothy, hugging her tight.

Dorothy heard the family step into the nearest coach. She squeezed Gram tighter. She heard train doors slam all down the platform. She buried her head in Gram's shoulder. The train's whistle blew.

Frank jumped out and yanked Dorothy aboard. The station guard closed their door and the train crawled forward.

Pressing her nose against the glass, Dorothy waved until her kinfolk disappeared. A few minutes later the city vanished. Mam handed Dorothy a small leather case. "Your present from Gram. You were too busy saying goodbye to notice it."

Dorothy opened the case. It was a sewing kit with small scissors, thimble, several needles and spools of cotton thread.

"You can keep up with your embroidery," said Mam with a wobbly smile.

"If I have time. Dad and Frank will need my help." Dorothy realized that Mam wasn't listening. She was dabbing her eyes with a handkerchief. Dorothy turned to the window.

The train sped through rolling green farmland divided into small fields by hedges and stone walls. When they arrived at Liverpool five hours later, Dorothy was famished. After Dad saw to the baggage, they had dinner at a nearby restaurant. Then they took a cab to Jackson's Boarding House for the night.

There were many grand buildings along the way. One had tall carved pillars. Another had a front garden with daffodils and primroses. Dorothy's neck ached from swivelling to see everything.

When they were shown their rooms at the boarding house, Dorothy tried out her bed. "It's soft as a cloud," she murmured, sinking deep into the eiderdown. Later the cloud grew hands and shook her. "Don't," she mumbled as her eyes flew open.

Mam sat beside her. "Gracious, Dodie, you've slept long enough. They're serving breakfast in fifteen minutes."

Dorothy snapped awake. "We're going to Canada now!" She skipped around in her nightgown.

Mam smiled. "Five minutes ago you were limp as a rag doll. You look sprightly enough now, so hurry and get dressed."

After breakfast the family took an electric streetcar to the dock. The landing stage swarmed with people and horse-drawn wagons. The air pulsed with honking, yelling and clanking sounds.

"Good grief," said Dad. "There are a thousand people ahead of us."

Dorothy grabbed his hand. "What if I lose you, Dad?"

Dad looked around. "Ladies," he said in a take-charge voice, "wait by that flagpole while Frank and I see to arrangements."

Dorothy, Lydia and Mam carried their hand luggage to the flagpole where the Union Jack hung limply in the damp air. With all the umbrellas milling about, Dorothy couldn't see the river.

She climbed a large crate and scanned the water, feeling like an explorer poised on the brink of the unknown. Dorothy had seen just such a drawing in a storybook. Her heart skipped when she spied a long ship with a black and white smokestack.

Mam looked up, aghast. "Good gracious, young lady! Get off that crate before you break your neck."

Dorothy scrambled down. "Our ship –"

"These are your travel clothes," interrupted Mam. "For heaven's sake, keep them neat." She smoothed Dorothy's skirt.

Just then Frank pushed through the wall of bodies. "Oh," he gasped, "I was afraid I wouldn't find you." He caught his breath. "There's a tug waiting to pull the *Lake Manitoba* alongside but the tide isn't high enough yet."

"Where's your father?" asked Mam.

"He went to the bank to buy Canadian dollars."

Mam paced back and forth. Finally she sat on somebody's trunk and took out her knitting. Dorothy sat on a nearby box and pulled Gram's present from her leather bag. *I hope I don't have to do much sewing in Canada*, she thought.

"Dodie, put that kit away before you lose it."

Dorothy squinted up at her sister, leaning against the flagpole. What was Lydia holding? She walked over to the flagpole and hissed, "And you had best hide that book before Mam asks who gave it to you!"

Lydia thrust the slim volume into her coat pocket.

Resettling herself on the box, Dorothy tucked her sewing kit away. She listened to snatches of conversation from people around her. A sobbing mother instructed her son to write often. That boy looked the same age as Frank. An older man promised to send for his family as soon as he got settled.

Finally Dad arrived with a bounce in his step. "The *Manitoba* docked a while back and they've been loading baggage. There's a fearful amount of it."

"I'm starving," said Dorothy.

Dad's eyes twinkled. "I thought you would be, my pet. I've brought scones and sausages for everybody." He passed around a paper bag. Everyone ate hungrily.

Suddenly a band struck up a lively marching tune. Excited sounds rippled through the crowd. People picked up their travel bags and pushed forward.

"If anyone gets separated," Dad said, "we're in cabin twenty-two. Don't forget your luggage." He grabbed Dorothy's bag and Frank took her hand. The Bolton family swept towards the narrow gangway.

Dorothy was crushed in the crowd. Strange elbows jabbed her and something knocked her head. She felt Frank's hand locked around her wrist, tugging her left arm forward. She clawed at a dark wool coat pressed against her face. She couldn't breathe.

Finally they stumbled onto the deck.

Frank squeezed her hand. "Are you all right, Dodie?"

Gasping for breath, Dorothy nodded.

Frank found a uniformed man and yelled in his ear for directions. Pushing through people, they found their way along a hall, downstairs, along another hall to cabin twenty-two. Dad and Mam were there, but no Lydia. Mam was pacing and wringing her hands.

"Don't fret, Aggie," Dad said soothingly. "Frank and Dodie found the cabin. Our Lydia will be here soon."

Lydia burst into the room, hat in hand and auburn hair tumbling down her back. "That was a madhouse," she cried, sagging onto a bunk.

Everybody breathed deeply and looked at one another. Then two deafening blasts filled the small cabin. Dorothy's hands flew to her ears.

Dad grinned. "We're pushing away from the dock. We're on our way to Canada."

Frank opened his diary. Dorothy peeked as he wrote with his new pen: *At last we are off and fairly on the briny.* "Now," he said, "let's explore the deck."

Mam settled herself on a lower berth. "I've found my bed and I'm staying put."

"I'll stay with Mam," said Lydia.

Dorothy jumped up and down. "Let's go, Dad!"

Mam frowned. "Such enthusiasm is very well in private, Dodie, but remember your manners in public."

Dorothy walked primly out the door with Dad and Frank. Their pace quickened along the passageway that led upstairs and out a wide, swinging door. Dorothy felt the deck vibrating underfoot with the thrum of the engine.

At the railing, throngs of passengers called farewell, waving handkerchiefs and hats. Dorothy squeezed through to the front. Now she could see a crowd on shore yelling and waving back.

The gap of water widened between the ship and the dock. The band on shore played "Goodbye Dolly, I Must Leave You," and two women beside Dorothy sobbed loudly. Everywhere she looked, grown-ups were sniffing and dabbing their eyes.

As the *Lake Manitoba* floated down the Mersey River, the buildings of Liverpool shrank to tiny blocks. The ship glided into a drizzly mist, fading the shoreline to eerie shapes. Most passengers retired to their berths.

"I'm going to get settled," said Frank.

Clinging to the railing, Dorothy stared at the shore. "I want to stay here."

Dorothy and Dad watched the river widen as it flowed out to the Irish Sea. A shadowy lighthouse blinked from the final jut of land.

"That's the last we'll see of England," said Dad. "Now it's full steam to Canada."

Dorothy's heart skipped a beat. Gripping Dad's hand, she stared ahead into the mist.

5

Aboard Ship

Too Jolly Ill For Anything

A bell gonged loudly.

A few minutes later, Lydia came on deck, shivering without her coat. "For Pete's sake, it's freezing out here. Didn't you hear the dinner bell?"

"Dinner?" asked Dorothy. "Good, I'm starving."

In the day room, people crammed together at long tables. Mam had saved three spots and ladled boiled potatoes and stew onto their plates. "There are many hungry people," she said. "If you're late you'll get nowt to eat."

"Where's our Frank?" asked Dorothy, spearing a potato with her fork.

"Frank is two levels below, travelling steerage," said Mam.

"What's that?" asked Dorothy with her mouth full.

Mam frowned at her breach of table manners. "Steerage is a big room where many people sleep. Our cabin has only four berths, so Frank couldn't stay with us."

Dorothy ate too fast to ask any more questions. She gobbled every scrap of food on her plate and had bread and jam for dessert.

After dinner Frank burst into the cabin, full of news. "What a frightful crowd in my hold. Three hundred men crammed together in rows of bunks. The *Manitoba* carried troops and horses to the Boer War. There are blobs of manure on the walls under the whitewash. The most beastly smell."

Seeing Mam's horrified face, Frank laughed. "The blokes around me are a friendly lot, already singing and playing musical instruments. I shall enjoy myself."

"Will you take me down there, Frank?" asked Dorothy.

Mam's expression shifted to a severe frown. "To the bedquarters of three hundred young men? Most certainly not."

"May Dodie help me search for our crates?" asked Frank. "The chap beside me said the baggage was pitched everywhere and the smashed boxes are woeful to behold."

Dorothy followed Mam's glance toward the porthole. The small glass window was dark. Night had fallen over the Irish Sea.

"I know," Dorothy sighed. "Bedtime."

"We'll explore the deck tomorrow, Dodie." Frank patted her cheek. "I'll go now to locate our baggage."

After Dorothy got settled in bed, Mam flicked off the electric light. Mam, Dad and Lydia withdrew to the day room. When they left, Dorothy climbed down from her bunk. She stared out the porthole at the sea, shifting and shimmering like black satin.

The next morning Dorothy emerged from a gently rocking dream. She opened one eye and saw Dad sleeping a few feet away. How could that be? Then she remembered; she was on a ship to Canada.

She scrambled down the ladder and stared through the porthole. A rocky shoreline gleamed pink in the sunrise. "I see Canada!" she shrieked.

In the bunk below Dorothy's, Lydia groaned and burrowed under her pillow. In the other lower berth Mam sat up with a start. Dad climbed down his ladder.

Wrapping his arm around Dorothy, he peeked out the round window. "That's Ireland, my lamb. Shall we go on deck for a better view?" Dad patted Mam's shoulder. "Sleep awhile, luv."

Dad and Dorothy wiggled into their clothes and tiptoed down the hallway. At the day room, Dorothy ran ahead through the swinging door into the damp salty air. Skidding on the wet wooden deck, she fell on her bottom with a thud. Someone laughed and Dorothy felt her face go hot.

"I say, that's a graceful entrance." Frank rose from a bench and pulled her up.

"What are you doing out so early?" asked Dorothy, straightening her skirt.

Frank waved to Dad, who had just stepped on deck. "Same as you and Dad, I reckon. Enjoying the spectacular view. Do you want to hear what I wrote?" They sat on the bench and Frank read aloud from his diary.

"We are rounding Ireland now. On our right is the coast of Scotland and on our left Erin's Isle and a beautiful place it looks, rising out of the blue water. The nearer points being brown and green and clear cut as though they had been washed clean by the storms of the Atlantic. The more distant points being purple-hued and shrouded in the morning mist."

Dorothy gazed at the shoreline. "That's exactly

right," she breathed.

Dad patted Frank's shoulder. "Did you find our luggage last night?"

"I surely did, Dad. In a big heap in the forward baggage hold. I couldn't see anything broke. Mind you," Frank added, "there was one trunk I couldn't locate."

"Is it the one with my things?" Dorothy asked urgently. "Did it get left behind?" She imagined her doll lying inside an abandoned trunk on the dock. Just like the real George, left behind in the cemetery. Shivers went up her back.

"Don't fret, Dodie-Podie. The missing trunk will turn up." Frank took her hands. "My goodness, you're shivering."

"A wind is coming up," said Dad, pulling his coat tighter. "Look at those swells."

For the first time, Dorothy noticed the ship was rolling. Staring at the waves made her dizzy. "Let's go inside," she said.

Waving goodbye, Frank disappeared through a doorway farther down the deck.

When Dorothy and Dad arrived at the cabin, Mam was dressed but Lydia lay curled up under her eiderdown. Dorothy stared at her sister's chalky face with grey lips pressed tight together.

"Lydia has the seasickness," Mam whispered, "and I only feel fair to middlin' myself. You two go to breakfast."

The tables were less crowded this morning. Dorothy ate a big bowl of porridge and several pieces of bread. Dad sipped a cup of tea. "I'm feeling a bit green about the gills," he said. Suddenly, he got up and ran out the swinging door.

After finishing her bread, Dorothy went outside to

investigate. She found Dad slumped on a bench, his face as pale as Lydia's.

Dorothy was horrified. Never in her memory had Dad been ill. "You look ghastly, Daddy. Will you be all right?"

"It's only the seasickness, Dodie." Dad managed a thin smile. "Go see how the ladies are faring."

Dorothy's heart pounded as she ran back to their cabin. Mam and Lydia both lay curled up sideways. Mam seemed asleep.

Lydia looked at her with glazed eyes. "Dodie," she said weakly, "find me a pail or something to retch into."

Dorothy looked frantically around the tiny room. Where would a pail be stored? She knelt and found two metal basins under each lower berth. The people who ran this ship must have expected everyone to get sick.

Lydia vomited into a basin, then lay gasping on the bed. "Oh, Lordy!" she moaned. "Don't just stand there, Dodo. Get me help!"

Dorothy bolted from the cabin. In the day room she found a man in a white uniform supervising the breakfast cleanup. A name tag on his lapel said *Head Steward: Curly*. Dorothy felt nervous approaching strange men, even in uniform. She swallowed hard, then forced her lips to move.

"Excuse me, Mr. Curly, everyone in my family is ill."

The steward's weathered cheeks crinkled into a smile. "Are they, missy? Don't fret, they'll get their sea legs in a few days. By the way, just call me Curly."

"You don't understand, uh, Curly. My sister is *deathly* ill. She..." Dorothy's lips froze in a grimace. It seemed too personal to describe what Lydia had just done.

Curly patted her shoulder. "Many people get seasick when they begin an ocean voyage." Dorothy stared at him, clenching her hands.

"I'll ask the ship's doctor to stop by," he added. "Which cabin is it?"

"Twenty-two."

Dorothy felt her face thaw and her hands relax. She sat and watched Curly bustle about, barking directions at the other workers. After a few minutes he left the room. She felt a knot of panic again. Had he forgotten her family?

Soon Curly returned, carrying a tray with two cups. Beside him walked a tall man holding a black satchel. Dorothy followed them to her room. Taking a paper from his leather bag, the man scanned the page until his finger stopped.

"You must be Dorothy Bolton," he said kindly. "I'm Dr. Smith. Get your coat and go on deck for some air. Your family needs to rest quietly for a day or two." The doctor opened the door.

The smell of sickness choked Dorothy's nostrils. She yanked her coat from the peg, then remembered Dad lying on the bench. She grabbed his coat too. Backing out the door, she heard Dr. Smith's voice, "Miss Lydia, I want you to sip some weak tea."

As she ran down the hall, Dorothy scolded herself. She'd forgotten about Dad until she noticed his coat. He must be cold outside. Maybe he needed weak tea too.

She stopped in the day room to button her coat. Through the window she saw Dad sitting on the bench talking to another man. She burst through the door and ran up behind them. "I'm glad you're feeling better!"

Dorothy skidded to a stop as the men turned to look at her. The man with black curly hair wasn't Dad. And he didn't look like he was better. Both men looked haggard and miserable.

Dorothy's joy crashed like a ball of lead. Clutching Dad's coat, she ran along the deck. She passed two women leaning over the railing. She almost tripped over a man sprawled on the floor. Frantically she yelled, "Dad, where are you?"

Between gusts of wind, she heard a whisper. "Dodie." When she heard it again, she peeked around a large wooden crate. There was Dad, sitting with his knees pulled up.

"Ahh," she exhaled, "I'm so glad to find you." She tucked his coat around him.

Dad forced his mouth to smile. "I found a spot in the sun, but out of the wind."

In the background the dinner bell rang.

"Shall I fetch you some tea, Daddy?"

Clenching his stomach, Dad groaned. "Mercy, no. I'm too jolly ill for anything."

Dorothy felt numb. She didn't know what to do.

"Don't trouble about me," he croaked. "Fresh air and rest are all I need. Go and eat." He clutched Dorothy's arm. "And remember Mam's rules."

There were empty spaces between the people sitting at the tables. Feeling lonesome, Dorothy wiggled onto the nearest bench.

"Hey, girl, is your family under the weather, too?"

A boy scooted down the bench to sit beside her. He looked a little older than her. He had light brown hair, freckles and an impish grin. "My mum and pop and big brother are all lying on their berths moaning." The boy demonstrated with a ghostly wail that sent Dorothy into a fit of laughter.

Helping himself to corned beef and boiled potatoes, the boy chatted. "They sound like those dogs chained up at the stern. Have you seen them? I'll take you after dinner. My name's Victor Sutton. I know yours is Dodie. I heard your family talking yesterday."

Dorothy gaped at him.

"Well, don't just sit there." Victor passed her the platter. "With everybody ill, there's twice as much for us."

Dorothy piled her plate high with food.

6

Aboard Ship
Up the Funnel and Into the Belly

After dinner Dorothy and Victor ran outside. Ireland had disappeared and the water was much rougher. They were in the open ocean. They clung to the railing, squealing as the ship rocked in the swells.

A man sitting nearby clutched his stomach. "Go away. It makes me even sicker to see you skipping about."

They tried to walk along the deck. With each tilt of the ship, they skittered between the inside wall and the railing.

Dorothy felt steadier after she grabbed Victor's hand. She had a fleeting thought that Mam wouldn't approve. That worry evaporated at the end of the deck when Dorothy saw the dog compound below. She clenched Victor's hand tightly.

"What a zoo!" said Victor gleefully. "Let's look at them up close." He pulled Dorothy downstairs and along the steerage deck.

Behind a metal barrier, a hundred dogs paced and pulled at their chains. Some strained towards other dogs, snarling and barking. A few animals lay motionless on the deck. When the pack noticed the children, the noise was deafening.

"Let's go back," Dorothy yelled in Victor's ear. After they retreated to the upper deck, she asked, "Is anyone taking care of those animals?"

Victor shrugged. "Probably not, with their owners ill."

"They aren't happy chained like that. Why did people bring them, anyway?"

"Pop says the poor blokes imagine themselves as gentlemen now they're getting land." Victor rolled his eyes. "They're bringing hunting hounds for their estates."

"I'm glad we didn't bring Chap. He'd be frightened of all the big dogs."

As they walked, Dorothy told Victor all the things they had left behind. She described how sad Lydia had been to lose her piano.

"There's a piano in the smoking saloon. I saw through the door when Pop went for a pint last night. Mum said he drowned himself in drink and that's why he got sick, but later she got sick too." Huffing out a sigh, Victor looked away. When he turned back he said brightly, "See the ladder going up the funnel? Let's climb it."

Shielding her eyes, Dorothy studied the smokestack gleaming in the sun. "Uh..." she hesitated.

Victor elbowed her. "You're not a sissy, are you, Dodie?"

Dorothy thought she might be, but she didn't want to admit it. "You go first."

At the base of a narrow staircase Victor slipped under a chain. Dorothy read the sign: *Crew only*. After a flash of doubt, she followed Victor upstairs to a small deck.

Darting over to the funnel, Victor began to climb. "What a lark!" he called down. "Come on!"

Dorothy clasped the highest rung she could reach. It felt gritty. *Mam will be frightfully cross if I get my dress dirty,* she thought. Putting a foot on the bottom rung, she started to climb. Every time she moved higher, her foot got tangled in her full skirt.

"Where are you?" Victor shouted.

Dorothy felt the wind whipping her clothes and her hair. "Right behind you," she yelled. She felt like an adventurer scaling a mountain cliff.

A deep voice blasted up like the ship's horn, "Get down this minute, you scamps!"

Startled, Dorothy almost lost her grip. With her skirt billowing, she couldn't see who was below, but the deck looked far away. She hugged the ladder in a wave of dizziness. Groping with her foot, she found each lower rung until she reached the bottom.

Curly stood there, scowling. "This is disgraceful behaviour, young lady," he growled. "The Reverend Mr. Lloyd shall hear about this." He hustled Dorothy and Victor down the narrow staircase and pointed to the sign.

"What does this say?" Curly glared at Dorothy.

"Crew only," she read in a tiny voice.

"And you, young scoundrel!" He yanked Victor's collar. "Are you part of the crew?"

"No, sir," said Victor, squirming.

"From now on, obey the signs. Now come and help lay the tables for tea." Curly strode down the deck muttering, "Unsupervised children will be the death of me." Dorothy and Victor had to trot to keep up.

At tea time Curly sat them far apart. "You'll be up to no good if you sit together," he said. The tables were half empty. Victor waved from his spot across the room.

Dorothy ate a boiled egg and several pieces of bread piled high with jam. She was drinking her second cup of milky tea when Dad staggered in and sat beside her. "I'm off to bed, Dodie," said Dad, after a few sips of clear tea. "How's our Frank?"

Dorothy inhaled sharply. She hadn't seen Frank since early morning. "I'll find out, Dad."

On deck she opened the door where Frank had disappeared earlier. With a fluttering stomach, she started down a long staircase. She arrived at a dimly lit hallway. Down here the ship's steam engine pulsed noisily like a giant heart. The air smelled foul.

Dorothy wanted to flee upstairs to the clean ocean air, but she had to find Frank. He might need a doctor. The hallway stretched left and right. Which way to turn?

She turned right and followed the hallway to an enormous room with rough canvas curtains hanging down both sides. The smell of sickness hung in the air, although she couldn't see any ill people. Children ran about noisily and a group of women sat at a long table. Farther down men sat smoking pipes.

"Are you lost, little miss?" asked one of the women.

"I… I'm looking for my brother."

"Is he married?"

"No," said Dorothy, coughing from the smoke.

Breaking into friendly laughter, the women called, "He ain't here, missy. This is the married quarters. Try the single men's hold, next level down." Some women pointed to the floor. Others motioned to the door behind her. "Keep goin' down the hall."

Dorothy retraced her steps. At the stairway she thought longingly of the fresh air on the deck above. Sucking in her lip, she kept walking until she found where the stairs went lower into the smoky gloom.

The next level had to be the bottom of the ship, far below the waterline. Clanking and throbbing sounds echoed up the stairwell. What was down there? An underwater dungeon?

Dorothy's head pounded. She pressed her hands against her temples to think. Mam had said two levels below. Frank must be down there! And she was the only one in the family well enough to find him.

Clenching the handrail, Dorothy descended into the belly of the ship. The staircase ended at another hallway. To the right was a closed door. To the left, the hall opened into a huge room reeking of smoke, sweat and other stinging smells.

At the doorway Dorothy's heart beat wildly. She took a step backward and bumped into a man carrying a mug of brown liquid. "Washa matter, little girl?"

Her mouth went dry. "I...I'm looking for my brother, Frank Bolton," she croaked. Thick smoke seared her throat.

The man stumbled into the room yelling, "Frank Bolton, Frank Bolton!" He motioned her to follow. Dorothy's cheeks flamed as she hurried past a table where men were playing cards, smoking and laughing. Some men in singlets slumped against the wall looking like they had the seasickness.

Rows of bunks stretched end to end, some with sleeping bodies in them. How would she find Frank? Finally she heard a faint voice. "Dodie." Collapsed on his bed, Frank managed a weak wave. Dorothy climbed over two empty bunks to reach him.

"Are you all right, Frank? Shall I fetch the doctor?"

"Aren't you brave to come looking for me." Frank squeezed Dorothy's hand. "The doctor's already been here."

"What did he say?"

"This sickness will pass soon. Now hustle upstairs before Mam finds out where you've been."

"Mam and Dad and Lydia have the seasickness too."

Frank forced a wan smile on his ashen face. "I guess you're in charge now."

Dorothy ran up the two flights of stairs to the deck. There was no one to tell her it was bedtime. She inhaled the clean salty air. Standing at the railing, she marvelled at the last glow of sunset reflecting from the clouds.

"Dorothy, bedtime!"

Storm lantern in hand, Curly patrolled the deck. Beside him stood a tall man wearing a bowler hat and black overcoat with a cape. "You could be washed overboard in the dark," Curly snapped, "and we'd be none the wiser." He opened the swinging door and shooed Dorothy inside.

"I don't want to go to my cabin," she objected. "It's too smelly."

"It's been cleaned. Now get to bed."

Frowning, the tall man stepped closer. Dorothy hurried away before he could speak.

That night she dreamt that waves grew as big as ·

mountains and crashed over the deck. Dad curled one strong arm around her, wrapping his other arm around a bench. Then Dad got the seasickness and couldn't hold on. An enormous wave swept Dorothy over the railing into the roiling sea.

Gasping for air, Dorothy clawed to the surface and woke up. She felt the swaying of the ship. In the dim light she watched the family's coats swing back and forth on their pegs. She climbed down and looked out the porthole. As the ship rolled, slate-blue water alternated with steel-grey sky.

"It's morning and I'm hungry," Dorothy announced to no one in particular. While getting dressed, she lost her balance and plopped onto Mam's berth. "Mercy!" she said. "The ship's really rocking today."

Opening one eye, Mam motioned Dorothy to lean closer. "I'm glad you're not ill, Dodie," she whispered. "Dress warmly if you go outside."

"I shall, Mam."

Dorothy yanked gloves, tam o' shanter and muffler from her leather bag and put them on. She pulled her coat from its peg and shrugged into it.

In the hall she grabbed the wooden handrail. By the time she reached the day room, Dorothy was used to the rolling floor. She ran toward the outside door.

Whssssst! A shrill whistle stopped her in her tracks.

Dorothy saw the tall man in the black overcoat stride toward her. He took the whistle from his mouth. "Are you Dorothy Bolton?" She nodded speechlessly.

"I am the Reverend Mr. Lloyd. Until your family recovers, you are in my charge."

Dorothy felt her mouth fall open. She closed it.

Mr. Lloyd pointed to a bench. "Sit and wait for breakfast."

Dorothy dragged her feet to the spot and sat. She laid her coat, tam, muffler and gloves beside her. The whistle shrieked several more times and children were ushered to seats well separated from each other. Dorothy noticed Victor across the room.

Finally Curly appeared with a pot of steaming porridge. A slight smile played at the corners of his mouth. "Behaving yourself today, Dorothy?" he asked.

After breakfast Mr. Lloyd gathered his charges. "It's too rough to play on deck. Go to your cabins and get something quiet to do in this room. Do not go anywhere else without an adult."

What can I do that's quiet? Dorothy wondered. When she packed her warm clothes back in the travel bag, she remembered Ada's writing paper. Groping through the inside pocket, she found the envelope and a pencil. She tiptoed from the room without waking anyone.

At a table Dorothy unfolded the two sheets of paper. She started to plan her letter: *Dear Ada...my whole family...*

Mr. Lloyd interrupted her thoughts. "Dorothy, I want you to mind Rose. Her mother is very poorly." He plunked a child on the bench and walked away.

Dorothy turned and saw a round face. The face had wispy blond hair, large blue eyes and lips pulled down in a pout.

"I want to draw a picture," Rose demanded.

"I haven't any paper to draw on."

48

"You do so. I see two papers." Rose snatched the pencil and started to scribble.

"Naughty girl!" Dorothy glared at the round face. "You've ruined my special writing paper."

The big blue eyes stared back. The pouty mouth opened. "I shall tell Mr. Lloyd you're calling me bad names."

Dorothy pressed her lips tight. *Little children are so beastly*, she thought.

7

Aboard Ship
Sea Legs

"Very well, Rose," Dorothy said through clenched teeth, "we'll share the paper. One piece each." Stuffing her sheet into the envelope, she pushed it out of reach.

"That's fair," said Rose. "Look, I'm drawing me." She worked intently, her tongue poking between her lips. Dorothy watched her form a lopsided circle inside the scribble marks. Then she drew four lines from the circle to the edges of the paper.

"What are those lines?" asked Dorothy.

Rose gave Dorothy a scathing look. "My arms and legs." Then she studied the drawing. "It's no good," she howled, sweeping the paper to the floor.

Dorothy shifted uncomfortably. If Mr. Lloyd returned, he'd think she had caused Rose's tears. "Pick up the paper, Rose," she sighed. "I'll draw a picture of you."

Rose's pout stretched to her chin. "You get it."

You lazy clod, thought Dorothy, bending to retrieve the paper. She laid the sheet on the table clean side up. Then she studied Rose's face. "Do you want to look as pretty as a princess?" Rose nodded.

Dorothy pulled a handkerchief from her pocket and

wiped two tears glistening on Rose's cheeks. "Princesses always smile."

Rose reworked her lips into a toothy grin.

"Perfect," said Dorothy, picking up the pencil.

When Mr. Lloyd returned later, Rose was curled up on Dorothy's lap. "Mr. Lloyd," she called, "Dorothy's telling me stories about princesses. See what she made?" She held up a picture of a round-faced girl with a wide smile and a jewelled crown.

Mr. Lloyd examined the drawing. "You have a pleasant manner with young children, Dorothy," he said. "After dinner, take her to cabin fourteen. Mrs. Thorpe will supervise her afternoon nap."

Curly and his helpers bustled about, laying plates and cutlery. Soon platters of fried cod and baked potatoes arrived. Dorothy cut Rose's food and made her a cup of milky tea. After dinner she took Rose's hand and walked to cabin fourteen.

"I don't want a nap," sulked Rose.

"Shh," said Dorothy as she knocked. "Princesses always nap. It makes them more beautiful."

"It does?" said Rose, perking up.

After a long pause a young woman with an extended belly opened the door.

"Dorothy says I'll be beautiful after my nap," chirped Rose.

"Thank you, Dorothy," said the woman, pushing straggly hair off her face.

Thank you, thought Dorothy, *for taking this royal nuisance back.*

When the door closed, Dorothy skipped down the

hall. She hoped Victor was still in the day room. There he was with other youths, clearing the tables under Curly's direction. When the cleanup was finished, Curly disappeared into the galley.

Dorothy surveyed the young people now seated at various tables. Approaching Victor, she whispered, "Do you want to visit my brother in steerage?"

"I surely do," said Victor, rolling his eyes. "It's been a ruddy bore cooped up here all morning. How many times can you read last week's copy of the *Boys' Own Paper?*"

"At least you didn't have a wretched imp to entertain. Come along, we don't need our coats. We'll only be outside for a minute." Dorothy led Victor down two flights of stairs to the door of the single men's quarters.

Victor exhaled a long whistle. "Now, this is a den of iniquity!" He grinned at Dorothy. "That's what Mum calls places she doesn't approve of."

"Mam wouldn't approve either," agreed Dorothy. "But I'm the only one who's not ill, so I have to check our Frank."

Dorothy led Victor directly to Frank's bunk. He wasn't there. A man leaned down from the upper bunk. "Blimey, two angels from above," he said. "Whadda ya want?"

"M...my brother, Fr...Frank," stammered Dorothy.

"He went on deck to...um...use the privy," said the man. He groaned and rolled out of sight.

Victor strolled over to a table where men were smoking cigarettes and playing cards. Dorothy plopped down to wait. Then she jumped up. Why was the bed so hard? She lifted Frank's blankets and discovered bare wooden planks underneath.

"Bit of a hard bed, what?" Frank leaned against the bedpost, trying to smile.

"Frank, you're better!"

"Slowly getting my sea legs." Frank took off his coat, rolling it into a pillow. "A few minutes of fresh air did me good."

Dorothy watched her brother lower himself onto the rigid planks. "Why don't you have a mattress, Frank?"

"Barr's letter promised there'd be bedding in steerage, but there wasn't any." Frank sighed. "At least, not in this room. So I'm sleeping on my wool rugs. Some blokes don't even have this much."

Frank closed his eyes. "Shouldn't you be getting upstairs, Dodie?"

"Mr. Lloyd said we had to be with an adult, and you're an adult, Frank."

"You've met the stately Reverend, have you? How about the short one, the scoundrel?" Frank's voice drifted off and he was asleep before Dorothy could ask him who the scoundrel was.

Dorothy looked around Frank's quarters. It was a forest of bunk beds. Coats and kit bags dangled from nails. Was that a gun barrel sticking out from a duffel bag?

Between bursts of laughing and yelling, she heard other sounds. Water sloshed beneath the rough floorboards. The ship's engine thumped energetically. Fiddles played in some far corner. Suddenly, high-pitched yelping tingled her ears.

"Dodie, come here," Victor yelled across several rows

of bunks. Something furry wiggled in his arms.

"What is it?" Dorothy asked, crawling across the intervening beds. She squealed when Victor held up a squirming black puppy. A young man sitting beside Victor had a puppy too.

"Two retriever pups, miss. Just weaned from their mother." The man looked at her with eyes as blue as a sunlit sky. Wavy black hair tumbled over his face as he leaned down to place the puppies in a wicker basket. He closed the lid over their yaps of protest.

"Patrick says we may come on deck with him to exercise the pups," Victor announced. Dorothy looked at him with pursed lips. "He's an adult," Victor assured her. "Aren't you, Patrick?"

"Aye, a full nineteen," said Patrick, pulling on a tweed jacket and cap.

"Well," said Dorothy hesitantly, "I don't have my coat –"

"Blessed Saint Mary, we can't have our little colleen catch a chill." Patrick ransacked his case. "Here's a jumper knit by me mother's own hand." He passed Dorothy a cream-coloured pullover with a cable-stitch pattern.

Dorothy felt unsure about wearing a strange man's clothes. On the other hand Mam would expect her to show good manners. "Thank you," she said, pulling the bulky sweater over her head. Patrick rolled up the dangling sleeves.

Dorothy followed Patrick up some stairs leading outside. She found herself on the steerage deck in the charge of a young man she'd just met. At the back of her mind Mam's voice nagged: *You went where? With a strange man? And an Irishman to boot?* But the puppies were so dear.

They ran from Victor to her and back again. They lapped water from a bowl and ate bits of cod Patrick had saved from dinner. When the pups tired, he tucked them in the basket and took them inside.

Cheers erupted from a crowd further down the deck. Victor grinned. "Let's see what's happening." He pulled Dorothy along, squeezing into the group.

The onlookers formed a large circle around two men who wore fat gloves and danced around each other, jabbing and punching. With every blow the audience hooted. Already one man had a bloody nose and the other a puffed eye.

Dorothy tore her hand from Victor's. She pushed through the ring of men and fled back to the door leading inside.

When Victor caught up she sputtered, "Why did everyone cheer? Those men were killing each other."

"No they weren't, silly girl. Have you never seen a boxing match?"

"No! And I'm not a silly girl. It was horrible! I'm going back to my brother."

"Ta-ta," said Victor. "I'll find my own way upstairs later."

After a deep breath of fresh air, Dorothy returned to the putrid steerage hold. Patrick and the pups were nowhere to be seen, so Dorothy left the jumper on his bunk. She found Frank sitting up, propped against the bedpost.

"I thought you had gone to your cabin," he said.

"No, I saw a boxing match on your deck." Dorothy grimaced with disgust.

"Boxing?" Frank's eyebrows shot up. "Dodie, you shouldn't be around things like that. You'll get in trouble with Mam."

And Mr. Lloyd, thought Dorothy. "I'd best go upstairs for tea, Frank. You look better."

Frank stood, then sagged back on the bed. "I guess my sea legs aren't fully formed yet." He wobbled a smile at Dorothy. "I want something to eat but I'm too weak to get to the table. Could you catch me a hard-boiled egg?"

Dorothy blinked. "Catch an egg?"

"Here comes the server now." Frank pointed to a man in a long white apron. The server clunked two buckets on the end of the table, which quickly filled with men yelling for food.

Leaning forward, the server immersed both hands into a bucket. His arms became a blur of motion, tossing and rolling small oval shapes towards the men. These objects spun through the air or wobbled unevenly along the wooden planks.

Dorothy ran over and nabbed two eggs as they slid by. The diners roared their approval and Dorothy giggled. Next the server tossed biscuits from his other pail. She stopped two with her arm as they skidded past. Dropping her catch into her pocket, she poured two cups of tea and returned to Frank's bunk.

Frank nibbled cautiously on his egg while Dorothy gobbled hers. She tried to bite into her biscuit. "How can you eat this, Frank? It's hard as rock."

"Yeah," agreed Frank. "The chaps here think the biscuits were baked before the Boer War. Went all the way to South Africa and back because the soldiers couldn't eat them either."

Dorothy stared at her biscuit. "They're that old?"

"It's a joke, Dodie. But they're awfully hard, even soaked in tea. I daren't try them; I'm afraid I'd break my teeth."

Dorothy collected the cups, eggshells and uneaten biscuits. "I ought to go now, Frank. Mr. Lloyd might be cross with me for having tea down here."

"Thanks, little sister. Your visit really cheered me up."

Dorothy beamed her warmest smile at her brother. She left the tea things on the table and bounced up the stairs.

Just as she reached the second staircase, a short stocky man in a clerical collar dashed by. Dorothy turned to stare at his back. He strode along the smoky hallway and disappeared down the lower stairs. *Who is he?* she wondered. *Why is he in such a hurry to get to the smelly bottom of the ship?*

Dorothy sprinted up the stairs, opened the door and breathed in the clean air. She skipped along the deck until a black coat stopped her. She looked up at Mr. Lloyd's frowning face.

"You have disobeyed me, Dorothy. I am disappointed in you."

Dorothy's cheeks burned.

"Where have you been?" Mr. Lloyd's eyes bored into hers.

"I...I visited my brother, Frank," Dorothy squeaked.

A severe frown froze on Mr. Lloyd's face. "You didn't tell anyone —"

"Excuse me, Reverend," a man called from the stairway door. Mr. Lloyd looked up. "Can you come to steerage and restore order? They're throwing biscuits at Barr."

"Can't that man take care of himself?" Mr. Lloyd muttered. He turned back to Dorothy. "Get to your cabin right now."

Dorothy nodded meekly and trudged inside.

At the cabin, Dorothy found Lydia brushing her dishevelled hair. "Where have you been?" Lydia shrilled. "Dad is looking for you."

Just as shrilly, Dorothy retorted, "I was down in steerage because..." She stopped. "Are you feeling better, Lydia?"

"Better?" Lydia burst into tears. "I want to go back to England."

"I mean, are you getting your sea legs? I could help you take a walk."

"I don't want sea legs!" ranted Lydia. "I hate this ruddy ship. If I could make it outside, I'd throw myself overboard."

Mam groaned in her bunk. "Girls, stop your row," she muttered.

Dorothy clamped her hand to her mouth. She tucked Mam's quilt around her shoulders. "Sorry, Mam. Go back to sleep."

"We didn't tell Mam you were missing," whispered Lydia. She stared at Dorothy. "Did you just offer to help me?"

"Yes," said Dorothy, meeting her stare.

Lydia ran her hands through her tangled hair. "Can you see if the bathing room is available?" she asked. "I would so like a bath."

Dorothy nodded and left the room. In a few minutes she reported, "It was occupied, but I knocked and somebody said to return in a quarter hour. I'll wait there and get you when it's time."

Lydia was lying down. "Thanks, Dodie."

With Dorothy's assistance, Lydia bathed and returned to the cabin. After dressing in fresh clothes, she fumbled to open the door.

"Shouldn't you lie down, Lydia?"

"No, I need to get out of here."

Lydia clutched the hand railing in the hall. Dorothy took her other arm and they hobbled to the day room. Sinking into soft armchairs by the window, they watched twilight fall over the rolling Atlantic waters.

"Do you fancy tea, Lydia? I can ask the Head Steward."

Lydia looked at Dorothy oddly. "Yes, I'd like a cup of tea. Thank you."

When Dorothy returned with the tea, Dad was sitting beside Lydia. She heard Lydia say, "It's the strangest thing, Dad. Dodie is acting so...thoughtful."

A warm flush tingled Dorothy's chest. *Lydia would never say that to me*, she thought, *but she must mean it if she said it to Dad.*

8

Aboard Ship
The Great Colonizers

The porthole glowed with silvery light; it looked like a misty morning. Dorothy stretched on her mattress, imagining Frank lying on those hard boards. Dad hadn't been cross about her visits to steerage. He agreed she had tried her best for Frank.

Leaning down, Dorothy studied Lydia, asleep in the lower bunk. She breathed softly through pink lips, not like yesterday when her whole face had been chalky grey. Dorothy was surprised how worried she'd been.

Mam was still asleep but Dad's bed was empty. He must already be on deck. Dorothy climbed down the ladder and got dressed.

Workers were laying the breakfast tables when Dorothy hurried through the day room. On deck she saw Dad standing with a man wearing an army greatcoat. They both stared intently at the wrinkled water.

Dorothy ran over. "What do you see, Dad?"

"Eleven o'clock!" he said excitedly.

Dorothy had just glanced at the clock in the day room. "No, it's only seven, Dad."

"A whale just breached." Dad grabbed Dorothy's shoulders, aiming her gaze to the left of the bow. "That

0

0

veteran said it's a humpback. There's its tail!"

Dorothy thought she saw a black V shape in the thin mist. She blinked. It was gone.

"Nine o'clock!" yelled the veteran.

Dad shifted Dorothy and pointed straight out from the railing. She inhaled sharply as a long sleek body arched above the water. Then a broad forked tail stood straight up before disappearing into the sea. They watched for several minutes but didn't see the whale again.

"Dad, what did the army-man mean when he yelled 'nine o'clock'?"

"It's a way of locating things around you that he learned in the war. You have to think of the ship as the face of a clock. The bow represents twelve o'clock and the stern six o'clock. So when he yelled nine o'clock, I knew where to look. Crafty, ain't it?"

After shivering awhile in the damp air, they went in to await breakfast. Lydia joined them, looking renewed with groomed hair and pink cheeks.

"You look pretty, Lydia," said Dorothy.

Surprise shot across Lydia's face. Lowering her eyes, she scooped herself a bowl of porridge. "And ravenous," she said.

"We just saw the most wondrous sight, Lydia!" "A whale jumped right out of the water!" Dorothy and Dad talked over each other, between bites of bread.

"One at a time," laughed Lydia.

Dorothy and Dad took turns retelling the story.

"I'm so looking forward to going on deck," said Lydia, "and breathing fresh air."

"Perhaps the whale will come back," said Dorothy hopefully.

After breakfast Lydia went for her coat and hat. When she returned, she said the doctor was visiting Mam. "He brought a tray and Mam tried a bit of porridge. We're supposed to stay away so she can rest."

On the way outside Dorothy noticed a poster tacked beside the door. *Volunteers requested for concert. First smoking saloon, Saturday night.* "Look, Lydia, that's tomorrow. You ought to volunteer."

Adjusting her hat, Lydia read the notice with a dubious look. "What could I do?"

"There's a piano in the smoking saloon. You know lots of tunes."

"Heavens no, not well enough for a public concert." Pushing the door open, Lydia stepped out. A gust of wind lifted her broad-brimmed hat and hurled it down the deck. With Lydia's shriek in her ears, Dorothy gave chase.

She captured the hat, snared on a coil of rope. "Our Frank's down here," she called back to Lydia and Dad, pointing to a bench further along. Grasping the hat tightly, she ran ahead to Frank. When she reached him she tried it on.

"Do I look like a proper young lady?" Dorothy mimicked Lydia's mincing gait.

Frank laughed. "If you let go, it'll blow away and Lydia will tear a strip off you."

"I'll hang on tight." Dorothy clutched the hat to her chest, rubbing her fingers across the soft blue velvet.

When Lydia and Dad caught up, Dorothy was listening to Frank read his diary. She wiggled over to make room on the bench. "Read the part about seasickness again, Frank. I'm sure Lydia will agree with you."

Nodding a greeting, Frank scanned the page and started to read. *"This seasickness beats anything I have ever had. It takes all the life out of you and makes you wish they would come round and pitch you overboard. The smell of food you simply abhor."*

"Oooh, stop reading, Frank," groaned Lydia. "I want to forget the last two days. It wasn't fair that Dodie didn't have a twinge of sickness." She snatched her hat from Dorothy's grasp.

"You weren't ill when I had the typhoid," snapped Dorothy.

"That truly was a bad time," said Dad. "We came so close to losing you, my kitten." He brushed back loose strands of hair that were blowing across her face.

Dorothy watched Lydia's mouth tighten. After an awkward moment Dorothy said, "I think Lydia should play the piano in the concert tomorrow night."

Lydia wrinkled her nose. "In a common place like a smoking saloon? Absolutely not." She arranged her hat and tightened the hat pins securely. "I'm chilled; so I'm going inside." Holding the hatbrim, she walked away as daintily as she could manage on the rolling, windy deck.

I hope I never act like that, thought Dorothy.

"Her airs are so tiresome," said Frank. "The wilderness will bring her down a peg or two."

"Have some understanding, Frank," said Dad. "The decision to emigrate has been hard on Lydia, and your mother too. I worry how they'll manage in the wilderness. You'll be a big help to them, Dodie."

"But Dad, I want to help you and Frank farm the land."

"Hmm," said Dad, "we'll see."

They watched Lydia lurch through the swinging door.

"Our Lydia hates this ship," said Dorothy.

Dad patted her shoulder. "Try to talk Lydia into coming to the concert. Maybe she'll enjoy herself."

Dorothy coaxed both Lydia and Mam to attend the concert. Arriving early, they got chairs and watched people cram into the room. Mam smiled approvingly when Dorothy offered her seat to a well-dressed woman. She squeezed to the front, joining Victor on the floor.

A man with a cockney accent sang. The adults laughed; Dorothy wasn't sure why. A woman with a mandolin performed several popular airs, off-key in Dorothy's opinion. Then a group of three violins played too long.

Dorothy's legs felt numb. The air was stuffy. She wanted to leave but there was no way to reach the door.

"My family's on the program next," whispered Victor as he got to his feet. His mother, Mrs. Sutton, took her sheet music to the piano. A taller boy, introduced as Charles, joined Victor beside the piano.

Now Dorothy's attention was rivetted. Charles and Victor performed several ditties, ending with "Two Lovely Black Eyes." After each verse Charles pretended to give Victor two black eyes. The audience roared with laughter. Dorothy thought they were wonderfully talented.

To end the evening, the announcer called on the Reverend George Exton Lloyd to say a few words. The audience parted respectfully as he stepped forward. Dorothy squirmed with the tall severe man looming over her.

"Everyone is invited to attend the Church of the Mid-Atlantic," he began. "Half-past ten tomorrow morning in this room. Remember, we need the Lord to lead us through the wilderness to the Promised Land."

Mr. Lloyd surveyed the audience approvingly. "Britons have ever been the great colonizers." His voice rose. "I see before me men of grit who will continue that fine tradition and take possession of Canada!"

As his voice boomed on, Dorothy wondered what 'grit' was. It sounded like something good to have.

Finally Mr. Lloyd nodded to Mrs. Sutton and she pounded the opening chords of a well-loved anthem. Dorothy knew the words from school and joined the crowd in belting them out. She was sorry when they reached the final refrain:

Rule Britannia, Britannia rule the waves;
Britons never, never, never shall be slaves.

Mr. Lloyd's talk had electrified the audience. Excited voices charged back and forth as people pressed through the doorway onto the deck. Dorothy wasn't sure what his words meant, but she burst with pride that she belonged to 'the noble British race'.

"That's why we're on this expedition, Aggie," said Dad enthusiastically, "to continue the fine British tradition."

"I thought we were coming for the free land," said Mam, rolling her eyes. "You know, Lydia, it was quite a mediocre concert. You could have shown most of them up."

"Except for Victor," insisted Dorothy.

"Music hall ditties!" scoffed Mam. "Victor is not a

suitable friend for you."

"Why not?" said Dorothy. "He kept me company when everyone else was ill."

Mam turned to stare at her. "Did Victor inspire you to talk back to your elders, Dodie? You know I cannot abide disrespect."

Biting her lip, Dorothy looked away. *I'll like whomever I choose*, she thought.

Dad took out his pocket watch. "Dear me, Dodie, it's very late." Directing Dorothy to bed, he continued down the deck for a stroll.

After Dorothy climbed into bed, Mam and Lydia lay together on Mam's bunk. Dorothy rolled to the edge of her berth and peered down enviously. She tried to listen but they were whispering too softly.

9

Aboard Ship
The Family Way

Dorothy awoke, still prickling from Mam's lecture. She peeked over her bunk.

Mam seemed to have forgotten her annoyance. She was intently grooming for her first public breakfast. Dorothy watched her twist long, chestnut-brown hair into a smooth bun. For the first time Dorothy noticed grey streaks.

By the time they arrived, the day room was bustling. "By gum, the tables are crowded!" said Dad. "Everyone is well again."

Dorothy waved to Victor, who squeezed against his brother and motioned for her to join them. "Victor's made room for me over there, Mam."

"You will not sit with that ragamuffin."

"You don't even know him," Dorothy mumbled angrily to the floor.

A gentleman shifted, making space at the end of a bench. On the other side of the table people moved and opened two spots. "Thank you, neighbours," said Mam, sitting down. "I'm Agatha Bolton and these are my daughters, Lydia and Dorothy."

Lydia smiled a greeting, tucking her skirt gracefully as

she sat. Dorothy plunked on the end of the bench. "There's no seat for Dad," she muttered in a stage whisper. "I could sit beside Victor and make room for Dad here."

Mam looked up at Dad who was nodding to a passerby. "Find a folding chair, Willy, so you can sit at the end." She shot a frown at Dorothy. "Save your breath to cool your porridge."

While Mam and Lydia chatted with the nearby guests, Dorothy stared at the varnished floorboards, tapping her foot. Her spirits rose after the food was served.

When Dad returned, Mam said, "This is the first breakfast we've eaten on board as a family." She served steaming oatmeal into four bowls.

"Except for Frank," said Dorothy, spreading jam on her bread.

"I'm sure Frank is comfortable in steerage," said Mam.

"Comfortable? Sleeping on bare boards, eating biscuits hard as rocks, breathing those awful smells?" Dorothy bit into her bread.

Mam's eyes narrowed. "How do you know so much about steerage?"

Dorothy choked, "Uh...uh...," The bread and jam caught halfway down her throat.

"Frank described the conditions yesterday," said Dad. "He told a lively story."

Dorothy took a long sip of tea. "Frank's a great storyteller, Mam," she agreed. "Ask him to read from his diary." She scooped a spoonful of porridge.

A sandy-haired man shuffled past, guiding a woman by the arm. She was dressed to go outside with a hat, gloves and a cloak over her large belly. Dorothy remembered her from cabin fourteen.

"Goodness," said Mam, "what is that woman doing on this ship? She looks very near her time."

"That's Rose's mum, Mrs. Thorpe," said Dorothy, watching them disappear out the door. She swallowed another mouthful of oatmeal. "What time is she near?"

Mam, Lydia and Dad looked down at the table.

Dorothy wrinkled her forehead. "What's that mean? 'Very near her time'?"

"I shouldn't have said that in front of you, Dodie," said Mam hastily. "It's a matter for grown-ups."

"But," Dorothy persisted, "Mr. Lloyd said she was doing poorly. Is she still ill?" She stirred her porridge while she thought. *What time is Mrs. Thorpe near?* She sipped her tea. *Oh mercy, not...time to die?* She bit into her bread. *Why won't anyone tell me what's wrong?*

The sandy-haired man returned inside, walking quickly. Dorothy jumped up and caught his sleeve. "Are you Mr. Thorpe? How's Mrs. Thorpe? Where's Rose?"

The man blinked, then a smile lit up his face. "You must be Dorothy Bolton. Is this your family?"

Mr. Thorpe smiled at Mam as Dorothy sat again. "Mrs. Thorpe suffered badly with the seasickness. We're grateful to Dorothy for minding our daughter the other day."

Dorothy enjoyed the flash of surprise on Mam's face. *And I've done more things you don't know about,* she thought mutinously.

Mam recovered enough to ask, "How is Mrs. Thorpe today?"

"Much improved, thank you," said Mr. Thorpe. "She

was eager to take fresh air after being confined so long."

"You must be relieved," said Mam, "considering her condition." Dorothy noticed the edge of disapproval in Mam's voice.

"Yes." Mr. Thorpe sighed. "I wanted to send for her and Rose later, but she insisted on accompanying me. She's a sturdy lass, but I do fret for her."

What are they on about? worried Dorothy. *What condition does she have?*

"Well, let us know if there's any way we can help." Mam sounded a bit huffy.

Mr. Thorpe brightened. "There is something," he said, turning to Dorothy. "Would you consider minding Rose for an hour? Mrs. Thorpe and I would be grateful for the opportunity to attend church."

"Uh...certainly," said Dorothy. Part of her felt proud to be asked. The other part groaned at the thought of an hour alone with that little pest.

"Come to our cabin around ten o'clock," said Mr. Thorpe. "We have toys to entertain Rose." He nodded to Mam. "I must be off. I left Rose alone in the room."

As Mr. Thorpe disappeared down the stairs, Mam fixed her gaze sternly on Dorothy. "Since when do you make arrangements with strangers without consulting me?"

Dorothy jabbed her spoon into her half-eaten clump of porridge and stared back. "Since we got on this ship!" she exploded. "Since you got ill! SINCE REVEREND LLOYD ASKED ME!"

"Keep your voice down," Mam hissed.

"Dorothy managed very maturely while we were laid

low with seasickness," said Dad. "Mr. Lloyd mentioned her skill at minding young children."

Mam's face softened. "Is that so? I'm sure the Reverend Mr. Lloyd does not give praise lightly." She smiled at Dorothy. "You may go to the Thorpes' cabin."

"Aggie," said Dad, offering his arm. "Shall we take a turn on deck before church?" Mam finished her tea and walked outside with Dad.

Dorothy glanced down the long table. They were the only diners left.

"You're lucky Mam doesn't know about your visit to steerage," whispered Lydia.

Dorothy's throat tightened. "You won't tell, will you?"

Lydia lifted her teacup. Her little finger curved elegantly in the air as she drank. She replaced the cup. "There's no need to get Mam agitated just yet."

"And I shan't tell about the book from your sweetheart," huffed Dorothy. "Just yet."

Lydia narrowed her eyes to green slits. "Right now we're even," she said. "Mind you, don't do any more foolish things."

"Foolish?" cried Dorothy. "Was it foolish to help our Frank?"

"It was foolish to go amongst rough men without an escort."

"Frank was my escort!" *And Victor and Patrick.* Dorothy decided to keep that thought to herself.

Lydia stood and gave her skirt a shake. The navy wool rippled into graceful folds. "I'm going to dress for church. You had best come with me."

"Lydia," said Dorothy as they walked down the hall, "why is Mrs. Thorpe's belly so big? Is she going to die?"

"Heavens, no," said Lydia, glancing over her shoulder. She lowered her voice. "She's in the family way."

"What do you mean? Does she have a tumour like Gramp?"

Lydia looked flustered as she opened the cabin door. "Mam will have to explain that." Keeping her back turned, she rummaged through her suitcase and pulled out long white gloves.

Dorothy stamped her foot. "TELL ME WHAT'S WRONG!"

Turning slowly, Lydia spoke through clenched teeth. "Control your temper, Dodo. You're not old enough to understand."

Rage steamed up Dorothy's throat like smoke spewing up the ship's funnel.

The door opened and Dad peeked in. "The Thorpes need you now, Dodie. They must get to the service early to secure seats."

Choking back anger, Dorothy walked out the door. At cabin fourteen, she composed herself and knocked.

As the door opened she heard a high-pitched squeal. "Dorothy!" A blond head squeezed beside Mr. Thorpe and two chubby arms circled Dorothy's waist.

"Rose," directed Mr. Thorpe, "let go of Dorothy so she can step inside." He looked at Dorothy. "I'm afraid she's a very energetic child."

Mrs. Thorpe struggled to rise from a wooden chair. "It's kind of you to mind Rose again. She talks of you constantly. I'm sure she'll be good for you."

Arranging a smile on her face, Dorothy said, "We shall be fine. Enjoy the church service." Mrs. Thorpe leaned on her husband's arm as they stepped into the hall.

Dorothy closed the door. This cabin was even smaller than hers. It had one set of bunks and a folding chair. There was no porthole. The single electric fixture cast sharp shadows. *I'm locked in a cage with a wild beast*, she thought. She summoned her most grown-up voice. "I hear you have some toys, Rose."

"Beside my bed, under there." Rose pointed beneath the bottom bunk.

Kneeling, Dorothy saw a small bed on wheels, low enough to store away during the day. Beside it sat a wide wicker suitcase.

Dorothy tugged the suitcase out and opened the lid. Inside were piles of neatly folded clothes, a large rag doll, some picture books and a tin box. Rose grabbed the floppy doll and bonked Dorothy on the head. Dorothy gripped Rose's arm. "I'm sure dolly doesn't like that. See the sad look on her face?"

Rose nodded. "That's Cinderella when she has to work all the time. But the other end is happy. Look!" Rose flipped the doll's long skirt, revealing another head beneath. "That's after she marries the prince."

Dorothy pulled down the satin side of the skirt to show a doll wearing a crown, a pearl necklace and a lady-like smile. "Princess Cinderella," she asked, "are you happy when Rose hits people?" Holding the doll's face to her ear, she announced, "Cinderella is happy when Rose acts like a princess, too."

"Oh, we can have a princess tea party!" Rose unlatched the tin box and pulled out two small wooden cylinders. She wrestled with the lids, whining, "They're too tight."

Dorothy pried off the lids and poured the contents on the floor. She examined the tiny wooden plates stacked inside. They were painted yellow. Someone had used a brush the size of an eyelash to add blue curlicues around the edges. The other cylinder, slightly thinner, contained matching cups and saucers.

"Shall we have tea and crumpets?" Dorothy asked.

When the Thorpes returned, she was reading *The Tale of Peter Rabbit* to Rose. Dad peeked in the door. "Come to the saloon, Dodie. Lydia agreed to play at the next concert if the family sings along."

Mrs. Thorpe thanked Dorothy while Mr. Thorpe unclasped Rose's arms from her waist. "Now, Rose, there will be another opportunity to see Dorothy."

"Whew," breathed Dorothy when she and Dad were alone in the hall.

"That child looks spoiled," said Dad. "I'm sure it was quite a job to mind her. Mam and I are proud of you for being helpful."

Glowing with pleasure, Dorothy followed Dad to the saloon where groups of people lingered after the church service. Lydia and Mam sat on the piano bench leafing through the new songbook from Gram. Dorothy peered over Mam's shoulder.

"What about this one?" said Mam. "It's about the ocean."

Lydia looked closely. "This song was in my other book. I've already practised it."

Poised over the keys, she started to play "My Bonnie Lies Over the Ocean."

Dad belted out the words in a booming baritone. Dorothy smiled proudly; she loved listening to Dad sing. Several men in the room held up imaginary beer mugs.

Afterward, Mam asked, "Willie, is this a pub song? I won't have Lydia play a pub song."

"I want to sing it," said Dorothy. "The words are easy."

"Come, Dodie," invited Dad, pulling her beside him. "Add your sweet high voice to mine." Dad nodded to Lydia, who played the tune again. Dorothy nestled against Dad's tweed jacket and sang with him. Afterward several people clapped.

With tight lips, Mam riffled through the songbook. "Here's a song we all know." She started to hum the tune.

"That's "Long, Long Ago"." We used to sing that with Gram," said Dorothy. "Oh, Lydia, please play it!"

Hunched over the music book, Lydia tried to follow the score. Dorothy winced at every wrong note. Lydia was even worse than the woman with the mandolin.

"Is this a family sing-song?" asked a familiar voice.

"Frank!" Dorothy tried to get his attention but everyone was talking at once.

"I was on deck with my mate, Patrick O'Reilly," said Frank, "and I recognized your voices." He called to Patrick, waiting at the door. "Come meet my family."

As Patrick shook Dad's hand, he winked at Dorothy. She wanted to ask about the puppies but she'd have to wait for a private moment. She noticed Lydia drop her eyes when she was introduced.

Patrick leafed through the songbook. "Here's an old favourite, Miss Lydia. Do you know it?" Looking at her he began to sing:

Drink to me only with thine eyes,
And I will pledge with mine;
Or leave a kiss within the cup,
And I'll not ask for wine.

Dorothy thought, *that's a silly song. How can you drink with your eyes?* She tried to smile at Patrick but his eyes were locked on Lydia's face.

When he finished he said softly, "I'll sing it at the concert if you'll accompany me." Dorothy watched a blush creep up Lydia's throat.

Frank took out his pocket watch. "By golly, Patrick, it's almost dinnertime. We'd better shake a leg downstairs." Lydia gaped at their backs as they left.

Dorothy longed for Gram, who played the piano expertly and always paid attention to her.

10

Aboard Ship:
A Long Way to Canada

The next morning the family went early for breakfast. As they got seated, Dorothy watched a burly
man with a large moustache stride toward their
table.

"Morning, Mr. and Mrs. Bolton," he said. "I'm Art
Sutton. My son, Victor, met your daughter the other day
while the adults were indisposed. Mrs. Sutton is sleeping
yet, but might the rest of us join you?"

"Certainly," said Dad, standing and offering his hand.
Mr. Sutton pumped Dad's hand. He beckoned Victor and
Charles over and introduced them.

Dorothy felt Mam stiffen beside her. *Mam's not
happy,* she thought, *but I don't care.* She beamed at
Victor who sat on her other side.

Victor whispered, "Have you been to steerage lately?"

Dorothy's heart skipped a beat. "Shh, Mam doesn't
know about that." She glanced quickly over her
shoulder. Mam was speaking across the table to Mr.
Sutton. Dorothy whispered back, "No. Have you?"

Victor nodded. "I saw the pups yesterday. Will you
come down today?"

"Uh...," Dorothy hesitated. She wanted desperately

to go, but how could she sneak away now Mam was better? Mam's voice cut into her thoughts.

"Lydia's just learning but she's made very good progress. And Dodie's going to sing, aren't you dear?" Mam smiled proudly in her direction. Dorothy nodded, moulding her features into a sweet look.

The servers arrived with bread, porridge and pots of tea. Dorothy nibbled out the centre of her bread and peeked at Victor through the hole. Victor sputtered with giggles into his cup of tea.

Mam whispered tersely, "Sit on my other side."

Reluctantly Dorothy moved to a cramped space between Mam and Lydia.

After they ate, Mr. Sutton said to Dad, "I say, ol' chap, have you read the *North-West Farmer* magazines that Mr. Lloyd left in the saloon?"

"No," said Dad, looking surprised.

Mr. Sutton slapped Dad on the back. "Come with me to the saloon. I'll fill you in." He looked at Charles and Victor. "You too, young men."

Dorothy sighed as Victor left. There had been no chance to discuss the puppies.

Mam's mouth thinned into a tight line. "I'm still a bit peaky from the seasickness so I shall return to the cabin to rest. I'll leave Dodie in your care, Lydia."

Lifting her teacup, Lydia nodded. "We'll get our coats in a minute so we can stroll on deck."

"I don't –" Feeling a kick under the table, Dorothy closed her mouth.

After Mam left, Lydia turned to her. "I want to go to the saloon to practise the piano right now."

"What about all the rough men in there smoking?" Dorothy tried to mimic her sister's disapproving voice.

"Our Dad's there now."

Dorothy looked at Lydia smugly. "Mam won't let you go."

"That's why I said we would stroll on deck, Dodo," Lydia snapped. Then her voice softened. "Actually, I do feel shy around all those men. Would you come with me? I want to practise the piece that Patrick sang."

A surge of jealousy boiled up Dorothy's throat. "I don't want to help you practise a song for Patrick!"

Lydia looked taken aback. "Why not?"

Dorothy cried, "I want Patrick to like *me*. I want him to show me the puppies again." After the words gushed out, she pressed her hand to her mouth.

Lydia looked even more surprised. "I didn't realize you knew Patrick. Well, he can like us both, can't he? Come on," she coaxed. "If you help me practise, I'll help you spend time with Victor."

Dorothy's pulse quickened. Perhaps she and Victor could visit the puppies.

Dorothy and Lydia tiptoed into the cabin to pick up their coats and the *Favourite Songs* music book. Outside the smoking saloon Dorothy peeked through the window. "Why, there's hardly anyone there. Just a couple of women reading on the couch."

"That's a relief," said Lydia. "I wonder where the men went?"

Dorothy pointed to a poster on the door. "They've probably gone to Reverend Lloyd's lecture on the steerage deck."

Lydia read aloud, *"Canadian Life and Problems."* She shrugged. "Dad can worry about that. At the moment my biggest problem is to play these songs without embarrassing myself."

Right, thought Dorothy, *you've got a lot of practising to do.* "Come on, I'll turn the pages for you."

The next evening, Dorothy watched Lydia brush her hair until it shone. Lydia looked at Mam eagerly. "May I put my hair up? I'm sixteen now." Dorothy was sure Mam would shake her head.

Mam studied Lydia for a long minute, then she smiled. "Your first concert is a special occasion." Opening her box of long hairpins, she expertly fastened Lydia's hair into a bun on top of her head.

"Oh, my," breathed Dorothy, holding up Mam's sterling silver hand mirror. "See how grown-up you look."

Lydia studied her hair, then she bit her lip. "I hope I don't make any mistakes."

"Don't fret, Lydia," Dorothy said. "We'll sing so loud nobody will notice."

The saloon was packed. After a week on ship with nothing to do, the passengers appreciated any entertainment. When the Boltons finally performed, the audience clapped and called for more. As Dorothy predicted, nobody noticed a few discordant notes. Standing between Dad and Frank, she felt very important.

Then Frank stepped forward, raising his hand for silence. "I'd like to introduce my mate, Patrick O'Reilly, who is well experienced singing in church choirs. He will perform a solo accompanied by my sister, Lydia." Patrick rose from the audience. Except for someone coughing, the room was completely quiet.

As he walked to the piano, Patrick winked at Dorothy. *He noticed me*, Dorothy thought, breaking into a grin.

Patrick nodded to Lydia and she struck the opening chords. Then his strong voice filled the room. Dorothy watched Lydia wince a few times but the audience didn't care. When the clapping faded Dorothy heard people murmuring: "Such a rich tenor...powerful voice...smooth as silk..." Her heart burst with pride.

After the Boltons returned to their seats, Mr. Lloyd ended the concert with a lecture about British respect for law and order. He declared that good manners would get everyone through these cramped conditions aboard ship.

What's he on about? thought Dorothy. *I always have good manners.*

As the crowd left, some people gathered in small groups to talk. Dad stepped close to Frank. "What has happened? Why did we get a sermon?"

Frank glanced toward Mam and Lydia, surrounded by a cluster of women. "Oh, that," he laughed. "How should I put it? Help me, Patrick." The three men stepped farther away. Dorothy moved close to listen.

"Well," said Patrick, "there have been several disagreements, of the physical type, down in steerage. Mr. Lloyd had to break them up."

Squeezing in tighter, Dorothy stared up at them. She felt Frank's hand on her shoulder. "Remember those hard biscuits, Dodie? After you left, we had a meeting with Barr about the poor food. Some blokes chucked biscuits at him."

Dorothy remembered the short man who had rushed

past her on the staircase. "I think I saw Barr. I didn't know he was even on this ship."

Patrick nodded. "Many people are angry about the living conditions aboard. They think Barr made false promises, so he's hiding in his cabin."

"Did the biscuits hit him?" Dorothy asked.

"One hit him on the side of the head," said Frank. "After that, he left in a hurry."

"Well," said Dorothy indignantly, "I don't blame Barr. Those men had abominable manners." That's what Mam always said when people behaved poorly.

Dad took Dorothy aside. "Dodie, remember to use your good manners. It's the Reverend Mr. Barr to you."

From the corner of her eye she saw Patrick step over to the ladies and whisper in Lydia's ear. Lydia blushed and another jolt of jealousy shot through Dorothy.

"He's still a man of the cloth, even if some people don't like him," continued Dad.

"Pardon?" said Dorothy, trying to focus on Dad's words. "Yes, Daddy, I'm sorry."

Dorothy fell asleep that night thinking about Lydia. She was proud of her, but she hated her; she wanted to be pretty like her, but she hated her.

The next day after breakfast Lydia asked, "Dodie, have you written to Ada?"

"No," said Dorothy, "and that nuisance, Rose, wrecked a sheet of paper Ada gave me. I only have one left."

"Shall we write letters home? I'll give you paper from my writing box."

"Thank you," said Dorothy, wondering why Lydia

was being so nice.

"Let's take our coats, in case we decide to go outside," Lydia said cheerfully.

They returned to the day room with their writing materials. Dorothy took the linen paper from Ada's envelope and began to write in her neatest script:

> Wednesday, April 8, 1903
> Dear best friend,
> It is a long way to Canada. Everybody in my family got seasick except me. I went to steerige to see if Frank was all right. He wasn't. Steerige is a big room with 300 men in it. Some of them have rough language.
>
> I met Patrick down there. Patrick doesn't have rough language. He has puppies. Patrick is wonderful, except he is sweet on my sister Lydia.
>
> Lydia played the piano at a concert. She made some mistakes. Nobody noticed because Patrick sang like a angel.
>
> Sometimes I have to mind a spoiled child named Rose, who is four years old. Her mother has a fat belly, like a big tumer. Lydia said she has the family way but she wouldn't tell me what that means. I hope she doesn't die because then I'll have to mind Rose all the time.

Dorothy studied her paper. Both sides were filled and she hadn't mentioned Victor yet. "May I have a sheet from your box, Lydia?"

Lydia nodded. "Shall I check your letter for spelling?"

"Uh, no thanks," said Dorothy. "I'm being careful." She started a new page:

> *I met a jolly boy named Victor. We climbed a ladder up the ship's funnel, just for a lark. I wish I was a boy so I could do more things like that. We got in trouble with the Head Steward but he didn't tell Mam or Dad.*

"Psst, Dodie." Lydia broke through Dorothy's concentration. "See Victor through the window?" Lydia pointed to Victor, leaning against the railing outside.

"I see him."

"Do you want to go down to steerage with him for an hour? I'll tell Mam we were strolling the deck together."

Dorothy looked at her sister suspiciously.

"You can see the puppies," Lydia said invitingly. "Just take this note to Patrick." Lydia held out a sealed envelope.

Dorothy pursed her lips. She didn't want to deliver a message from her sister. On the other hand, she longed to see those dear pups. After folding her own note into its envelope, she took Lydia's letter. She stuffed both envelopes into her dress pocket.

Lydia passed Dorothy her coat. "Just one hour. I'll wait on the bench outside."

Dorothy scooted outside and tugged on Victor's grey Norfolk jacket. "I may visit steerage for an hour to see the puppies."

"Jolly good! Let's go." At the stairs leading to the steerage deck, Victor scanned the crowd below. "There's

Patrick with Frank!"

Following Victor's pointing finger, Dorothy located two men sitting against a crate. The pups scrambled over their laps. Dorothy ran downstairs with Victor at her heels.

When the dinner bell gonged, Dorothy gasped. "I've been far longer than one hour. Lydia will be so cross." She handed her puppy back to Patrick and ran upstairs.

Lydia sat on the bench with tightly folded arms. "Have you no sense of time?" she fumed. "What did Patrick say when you gave him the note?"

"Uh..." started Dorothy. Lydia's envelope was still in her dress pocket. She felt it smoldering like a hot ember.

"You little wretch! You didn't deliver my note!"

"Yes, I did," Dorothy said weakly.

"You did not, liar. I can tell by your face." Lydia pointed to the stairs. "Get down there and give it to Patrick. I'll wait right here."

By the time Dorothy got downstairs, the men had gone inside. She couldn't see Patrick at the crowded tables, so she left the letter on his bunk. She flew back upstairs where Lydia waited with a wicked scowl.

"I delivered your precious letter," cried Dorothy and ran in for dinner. She kept her distance from Lydia for the rest of the day.

Thursday morning, Dorothy awoke to Dad's hand nudging her shoulder. He had his coat and hat on. "There's something wondrous in the water, Dodie. I'll meet you on the forward deck."

Dorothy sat up. "Is it the whale again?" Dad had already left the cabin. She scrambled down the ladder and tugged on her woolen stockings. She thrust her feet into her dainty Sunday shoes, tossed her coat over her flannel nightgown and hurried out the door.

Dorothy pushed through the crowd to the railing. Some way ahead a ghostly grey mountain sat in the ocean. Once she found her wits, she shrieked, "An iceberg!"

"Tha' be so, lassie," agreed a man in a thick Scottish brogue. "About a mile off, I reckon. Our ship be steering a wee bi' to starboard, else we'd crash into it."

There wasn't a breath of wind. The ship glided forward on the glassy sea and the ice mountain grew larger. The ice glowed with shades of turquoise, green and blue, luminous tints of colour Dorothy had never imagined before.

"I wish we could sail right beside it," she said.

"Nae, lassie, we dinna wan' to do tha'," said the Scot. "Icebergs be treacherous."

The crowd watched as the gigantic body of ice slid past like a stately ship.

"Well, I'll be," laughed a gentleman with a pair of opera glasses. "The iceberg has passengers, too." He passed the binoculars around but nobody thought to give Dorothy a turn. She watched longingly as a lady in a fur coat handed the glasses back to their owner.

Finally Dorothy blurted out, "What kind of passengers are on the iceberg?"

The Scot looked down in surprise, "Did ye nae get a turn, lassie?" He looked around for the gentleman but it was too late. The man had gone. "Well, lass," the Scot said kindly, "It be a flock o' birds, standing in a row like sailors lined up for inspection."

"Really?" said Dorothy, squinting at the iceberg receding into the distance. She thought she could see a line of tiny black dots.

She found Dad and put her arm through his. "What wondrous miracles we're seeing on this ocean," said Dad. They stood together, staring at the immense mirror of the sea. Pink-edged clouds seemed to float in the water.

Dorothy shivered and Dad opened his overcoat, pulling her against his warm body. He wrapped his coat tightly around her.

"Snug as a bug in a rug," giggled Dorothy. Then she felt a wave of sadness. That's what Gram always said when Dorothy stayed overnight and Gram tucked her into bed.

"I miss Gram," she said wistfully. "And we've only been gone a week."

"I know, my lamb," said Dad. "But you'll always have Gram's love in your heart."

Dorothy felt tears spill out. Unwrapping his arms, Dad fumbled in his coat pocket. He handed Dorothy a handkerchief. As she wiped her eyes, Dorothy sighed, "It's a long way to Canada, Dad. Will we ever get there?"

"The iceberg is a sign," said Dad. "We must be near."

Dorothy's heart fluttered. What would the mysterious pink country be like?

11

Aboard Ship

The End of the Journey by Sea

The next day more signs showed that Canada was near. Dr. Smith held a clinic for those who had neglected to get smallpox vaccinations in England. A poster announced: *Canada will not admit anyone without a vaccination scar.*

Dorothy saw Victor waiting in line for a needle. She waved sympathetically, remembering how her arm had ached for days.

After dinner everyone assembled on deck on the order of the ship's purser. The cabin-class deck was packed.

Dorothy was jammed against the railing. She surveyed the far larger crowd crammed on the steerage deck. All she could see was a mass of flat caps: black, grey, brown and checkered. Climbing the railing, Dorothy leaned over for a better look. Now she could see a steward checking a list as one person at a time stepped inside.

"Good gracious, Dodie, get off that rail!"

Dorothy jumped down and turned around.

Mam was smiling. "I'd prefer you to be alive when we reach Canada."

"You sound happy, Mam."

"Indeed," said Mam, "I'll be blessed happy to get off

this madhouse."

When the crowd thinned, the Bolton family lined up at the door. Soon it was their turn to be checked off Curly's list as Dad announced their names. "Hi Curly," said Dorothy, but he was too busy to answer.

Inside the day room people buzzed with excitement. "Will Bolton, did you hear the captain's announcement?" Mr. Sutton gave Dad a friendly slap on the back. Mam and Lydia stepped closer to listen.

Dorothy patted Victor's arm to get his attention.

"Ow!" he winced, pulling away.

"I'm sorry! I forgot you just got vaccinated."

"Yeah," grumbled Victor, "Mum and Pop thought children didn't need one."

"Don't fret," said Dorothy cheerfully. "It'll feel better by the time we reach the North-West Territories."

"What?" squawked Victor. "We have to spend a week on the train first. It ruddy well better stop hurting before then."

Who's the sissy, now? thought Dorothy. "I was just joking, Victor. It'll feel better tomorrow."

Mam turned, giving Dorothy a quick hug. "Let's go and pack!" she said.

"Are we almost there?"

"We shall be in Saint John by noon tomorrow." Mam steered Dorothy down the stairs and did a quickstep along the hallway. Dorothy blinked; she had never seen Mam act so giddy.

Later the family went for a stroll on deck. A keen wind caused swells to beat against the ship's hull. Dorothy pulled her tam o' shanter down over her ears.

"Strange," said Lydia, tightening her head scarf. "The rocking of the ship made me seasick for days but it doesn't bother me now."

"What doesn't kill you makes you stronger," declared Mam. "Thank heaven we're only going one way," she added. "I couldn't survive another bout of that seasickness."

"Victor said we'd be on the train for a week," said Dorothy. "How can that be, Dad? Is Canada as wide as the ocean?"

"I'm afraid so," said Dad. "It's over two thousand miles to the North-West."

"Let's not think of that now," said Mam in a sprightly voice. "It's almost teatime. Shall we make ourselves comfortable on those soft wooden benches?"

Dorothy grinned. There seemed no end to Mam's good spirits.

After tea, Frank visited the cabin. "How are the puppies, Frank?" asked Dorothy. "May I see them again?"

"Many times," said Frank. "Patrick and I have talked about sharing the pups." He looked at Mam and Dad. "Actually, we're planning to get adjoining homesteads and share one house on the property line."

Mam's face went pale. "You won't live with us, Frank?"

Dorothy's heart jumped into her throat. *Not live with the family?* She pinned her eyes on Frank's face.

"Frank," said Dad in a low voice, "we'll discuss this on the train." He added cheerfully, "Let's go on deck to enjoy our last evening at sea."

They reached the bow just as a cheer went up from people gathered at the rail. Dorothy wiggled through the crowd. Someone pointed. "Look, miss, a lighthouse on the southern tip of Nova Scotia."

Against the deepening red sky, Dorothy saw a blinking white light. "Canada!" she cried. In the excitement she forgot her distress about Frank.

Dorothy could hardly wait to see her new country. But the next morning was cold and foggy. Only misty impressions of land were visible on both sides of the ship. It didn't look anything like the wide pink map Miss Davis had shown her.

After breakfast the family lingered over their tea. They watched curiously as kitchen workers set out mountains of freshly baked bread.

Dad went to read a notice on the wall. His moustache twitched as he returned to the table. "We must supply our own food on the train. Mr. Barr ordered eight thousand loaves to sell to the colonists for the trip. But he's asking an outrageous price."

"Where shall we get enough food for a whole week?" asked Lydia.

"The notice says we can buy supplies whenever the train stops at a town."

"Hm," said Mam, "I can't imagine a small town bakery having enough bread for two thousand people. We'd best buy some bread here."

"At tuppence hapenny each?" said Dad indignantly. "That old rogue, Barr, is trying to make money off us."

Dorothy inhaled deeply. "They smell delicious, Dad."

"A bird in the hand is worth two in the bush," said Mam. "Buy four loaves, Willy."

Dad reluctantly passed ten pence to the clerk. Dorothy and Lydia each tucked two loaves under their arms. "But we can't eat only bread for a week," said Dorothy.

Dad looked out the window while he considered Dorothy's point. "There's Art Sutton outside. He's a practical fellow. I'll ask what he's planning to do."

"Well, young ladies," said Mam, "shall we return to the cabin and tidy up for our introduction to England's largest colony?"

An hour later Dad came to the cabin. "We're anchored in the Saint John harbour, but we can't dock until the quarantine flag is lowered. Government doctors have come on board. They'll check everybody's vaccinations after dinner."

Dorothy blinked. "After dinner? Shan't we be on shore by then?"

Dad sighed. "Bad news, I'm afraid. We can't disembark until tomorrow."

After dinner, the cabin-class passengers assembled on deck and were allowed into the day room by family. Dad disappeared behind a screen. A nurse with a starched apron ushered Dorothy, Mam and Lydia into a curtained booth.

With a flushed face, Mam unbuttoned her blouse to expose the vaccination mark on her upper arm. Her fingers fumbled unbuttoning the back of Dorothy's dress. Lydia stared at the ceiling while the nurse examined her arm. The nurse marked their names off a passenger list and certified them safe to enter Canada.

Dad was waiting. "I'm glad Canada is so concerned with health," he joked.

"Do you get sent back to England if you don't have a scar?" asked Dorothy.

"They keep the whole ship under quarantine until everyone is vaccinated."

"Oh," said Dorothy, "I'm glad Victor got his done yesterday."

Later, two Canadian bankers set up office and Dad bought a bag of coins. At the cabin Dad opened the pouch and handed Dorothy a disc of shiny copper. She turned it over in her hand. One side had a profile of King Edward. The other side said, *"one cent 1902"*, inside a wreath of leaves. She passed the coin to Lydia.

Mam examined a silver piece. "Our dear departed queen," she said quietly. Dorothy snuggled next to Mam to look. This coin had a profile of Queen Victoria and the date 1899.

Dad studied a paper explaining the coins' values. "That's a quarter. It's worth a bit less than a shilling." He gave Dorothy a smaller silver coin, stamped with *10 cents*. "This is a dime. Keep it in your pocket and buy some Canadian stamps from Mr. Lloyd."

The dime gleamed like a jewel in Dorothy's hand. "Buy stamps?" she echoed.

"Yes," he said. "I noticed Mr. Lloyd purchasing sheets of stamps from some official. He said he would sell them at teatime."

"Oh," exclaimed Dorothy, "I had best finish my note to Ada."

Dorothy ran to the day room with her unfinished letter. *So much more has happened*, she thought, *and I only have a bit of paper*. She sat down and continued:

Dad and I saw a iceberg. Lydia is too lazy to get

*up early so she missed it. The iceberg looked like a
giant castle. It had birds on top but I couldn't see
them very well.*

*Yesterday Victor got a small poks vacsination.
He had to because nobody can leave the ship if
some body isn't vacsinated. Today we had to show
a nurse our scars. It was embearacing to undress
even though we went behind a curtain. Lydia was
blushing.*

*We still have to go two thosand miles on a train.
I'm afraid we shan't have enough food. I hate being
hungry.*

Your best friend, Dodie Bolton.

Dorothy squeezed her signature on the bottom. She
folded both pieces of paper into the envelope and studied
Ada's address: *962 Old Newton Street, York, England.*
That seemed so far away now.

As she watched people exchange money at the
bankers' table, Victor sidled up and nudged her. Dorothy
pulled the shiny dime from her pocket. "Look," she said
proudly.

"That's not much," said Victor, wrinkling his freckled
nose. "I earned a quarter tending a gentleman's dog
during the trip."

"Well," retorted Dorothy, "it's enough to buy
stamps." She noticed Mr. Lloyd arranging items on an
empty table and strode over to him.

"Hello, Reverend Lloyd," she said shyly. "May I buy
some stamps?" She held out the dime and her letter.
"And will you post this to my best friend?"

Mr. Lloyd examined her letter before sealing the

envelope. "I see you take your penmanship seriously, Dorothy. You have a very neat script."

"Uh...uh, thank you." Dorothy felt flustered. No one had ever complimented her handwriting before. But she'd never written a real letter before, only those tedious exercises at school.

"Shall I put a return address so your friend can write back?" Dorothy nodded and Mr. Lloyd wrote: *Dorothy Bolton, c/o Barr Colony, Saskatoon, District of Saskatchewan, Canada.*

"Is that where we're going...Sas, Sas-ka-toon?" Dorothy tripped over the unfamiliar word.

"We go by steam to Saskatoon. Then we'll strike out across the prairie in wagons." Mr. Lloyd affixed a two-cent stamp to her letter and dropped it into the mail basket. "Here," he said, "four stamps for future letters."

"I don't have any more writing paper," sighed Dorothy.

"Don't you?" said Mr. Lloyd. He handed her two sheets of paper and an envelope. "I'm sure you have a nice auntie or grandma back home."

"Oh, thank you. I shall write to Gram after tea."

Dorothy was happy to be busy that evening since everyone else was grumbling about the delay. Mam's good spirits had fallen. Even Dad seemed depressed.

The next morning after breakfast, Frank came to the cabin with his travel bag. "Do you want to hear what I wrote in my diary last night, Dodie?"

Dorothy nodded. Frank opened his leather book and started to read.

"The houses on the top of the hill were silhouetted against

the colored sky. As it gradually gets darker the lights begin to twinkle here and there and before long the whole bay is dotted with twinkling lights. We turn in tonight feeling sorry that we are not sleeping in the train and yet glad that we have come to the end of our journey by sea safely."

"Amen to that," said Dad.

"And this is Easter Sunday," said Mam. "A day to be glad for many things."

Dorothy felt the floor vibrate. Humming and clanking sounds started. She suddenly realized those familiar sounds had been quiet while they were at anchor.

"We're landing at last!" Grabbing her coat, she flew out the door.

She faintly heard Mam call, "Slow down and walk properly." A minute later Frank and Dad ran after her.

They watched the ship draw up to the dock. Sailors threw strong cables to men on the landing stage who wrapped them around thick posts. Wooden chutes were pushed up to openings in the hold and baggage started tumbling down to the dock. One crate split apart when it landed and the men pushed it aside.

Dorothy cried, "They're being very rough with the luggage."

"There was some frightful destruction in the baggage hold," said Frank. "I pray our things come out safely."

Dorothy closed her eyes and prayed for George.

12

April 12, 1903

Off the Ship

Dorothy watched crates and steamer trunks crash down the chutes. A trunk popped open, spilling its contents onto the dock. The closest worker kicked the objects back inside and snapped the lid shut. Dorothy gasped as a yellow parasol rolled into the water.

"Don't fret, Dodie," said Dad. "Our trunks are covered with iron sheeting and secured with leather straps. They ought to hold. Heaven knows I paid enough for them."

"Look!" Dorothy pointed to a line of men crossing the gangway. "I'll tell Mam and Lydia it's time to go." She ran to the cabin and flung the door open. "Grab the bags!"

"Hold your horses, Dodie," panted Frank, close on her heels.

"The first train is loading," Frank said to Mam, "but it only goes to Winnipeg."

What's Winnipeg? Dorothy wanted to ask, but Frank was still explaining.

"Some blokes are worried that they have no farming experience. Last night a government man promised to find them work in Winnipeg."

"Did...Patrick disembark?" asked Lydia, trying to sound casual.

"No, dear sister," said Frank. "Patrick is determined to homestead at the Barr Colony." Frank glanced at Mam, who was packing something in her bag. He dropped an envelope in Lydia's lap and she quickly tucked it away.

Dorothy was still staring at Lydia's pocket when Dad arrived.

"We're on the third train," he said. "We disembark after teatime. Art Sutton and I are slipping off the ship to purchase provisions. The rest of you go to dinner." Dad checked his wad of dollar bills and grabbed the bag of coins.

Dorothy wished she could go exploring with Dad. Instead, she had to sit quietly at dinner, squeezed between Mam and Lydia.

After the meal Reverend Lloyd announced that the second train would load immediately. At two o'clock he would hold Easter service for the remaining passengers. Dorothy groaned. It wasn't fair to be stuck on board singing hymns when other people were setting foot in Canada.

At the cabin Mam and Lydia arranged their wide-brimmed flowered hats. "Thank heaven for Mr. Lloyd," said Mam. "I was feeling rather sinful not worshipping at Easter."

Mam inspected Dorothy's green plaid dress, shaking out the skirt. "A bit wrinkled, but it'll have to do," she said. "It's the only clean frock left." She plunked a straw sailor hat on Dorothy's head, snapping the elastic under her chin.

"Ouch," said Dorothy. She wiggled her feet into the patent leather shoes that were only for church.

The steerage deck was crammed with people dressed in their Sunday best. Mam and Lydia found seats, but Dorothy was shunted off to the side in a crowd of children. Victor nudged her. "When the service starts I shall sneak off for a look at Saint John. Do you want to come?"

Dorothy's mouth dropped open. "Sneak away from church? Leave the ship?"

"We'll be back before church is finished." He held up his quarter. "I'll buy you a treat."

She stared at him incredulously.

"You're such a goody two-shoes," snorted Victor. "I'll go alone." Dorothy watched him slip through the doorway leading downstairs to Frank's hold.

The crowd hushed as Reverend Lloyd's booming voice began, "Beloved of God, we are now halfway to the Promised Land..."

Not another sermon about the Promised Land, thought Dorothy. *What about the promise to get off this ship?* Ducking behind the children, she dashed downstairs and flew through Frank's quarters. The room looked barren without bedrolls and kit bags. She raced upstairs to the cabin deck and caught Victor as he crossed the gangway.

"Wait for me!"

Victor grinned. "Hurry. We only have an hour." They squeezed between crates on the landing stage and ran past storage sheds overflowing with baggage.

At the end of the dock they found a trail cut into a grassy embankment. Dorothy wobbled along the path. "The ground feels too hard," she said.

Victor laughed. "It surely does. We'll get our land legs in a minute."

By the time they reached a wooden staircase, the ground felt normal. They ran up the steps to a paved street running parallel to the shore. Three-storey brick buildings edged the street but all were closed. Dorothy and Victor stood still on the empty street.

I'm in Canada, Dorothy thought, tapping the pavement with her shoe.

"There's gotta be a couple hundred men from the ship buying supplies," said Victor. "If we're quiet perhaps we'll hear them."

All Dorothy heard were seagulls cawing overhead and small boats creaking against a dock. Slowly her ears tuned to faint human sounds. She pulled Victor to the next side street, where a crowd milled about two blocks away.

Victor whistled. "You've got sharp ears, Dodie."

He tore down the street and Dorothy ran like the dickens to keep up. She wished she were wearing her everyday laced boots instead of these flimsy Sunday shoes. They skidded to a stop under a red-and-white awning and glued their noses to the store window.

"It's so crowded I can't see what they sell," said Dorothy.

"There's jars of sweets on a shelf behind the counter," said Victor. "Shall I buy some licorice?"

"I love licorice, but let's see what else they have."

"Dodie, there are only men inside," said Victor uncertainly. "Shall you wait here while I buy us something?"

Dorothy looked at him disdainfully. "Certainly not.

I'm very experienced at making purchases in a shop."

She marched through a group of men conversing outside and opened the glossy red door. Victor followed her. A tinkling bell announced their entry, but nobody noticed. Pushing up to the counter, they stared at jars of sweets. The jars were labelled: peanut brittle, licorice sticks, peppermint sticks, lollies, toffee, Tootsie Rolls.

"Tootsie Rolls," read Dorothy. "What are they?"

"I don't know," said Victor. "Let's buy some." He waved his quarter, trying to get the eye of the man at the cash register. A shopper with an armful of apples, a slab of cheese and two brown paper bags elbowed in front of him.

"Look at the bloomin' queue waiting to pay," said Victor.

Dorothy glanced around. "See that tall girl at the barrels. She must be the shopkeeper's daughter. I'll ask her for help while you stand in the queue."

The girl was scooping brown things into paper bags and weighing them. She smiled as Dorothy approached. "Do you wish a pound of dates? Fifteen cents."

"Half a pound, please," said Dorothy, "and some licorice and Tootsie Rolls."

The girl pushed strands of hair off her face. "Show me your money."

Dorothy pointed to Victor. "My friend has a quarter." The girl took the quarter and returned with a small brown bag.

"What did we buy?" asked Victor as they pushed out the door.

"Licorice and Tootsie Rolls and dates."

"What?" exclaimed Victor. "You spent my hard-earned money on dates?"

"I had to buy dates to get her attention. Stop complaining. You'll like them."

They sat on the front step of Dumont's Dry Goods Shop next door. It was closed but Dorothy noticed bolts of cloth, hats and feather boas through the window.

"Crikey!" said Victor, smacking his lips. "Tootsie Rolls are tasty." He handed Dorothy a small wrapped cylinder.

She peeled off the wrapper and looked at a brown lump about the size of a date. She popped it in her mouth. As she chewed, she tasted hints of cocoa and molasses. "Delicious," she agreed. She reached into the bag. "Do you like my moustache?" she asked, curling her upper lip around a stick of licorice that stuck out on both sides.

Victor bent a licorice stick and bit the middle. The black ends protruded from his mouth. "Fangs," he said.

Laughing, Dorothy broke her licorice in half and tucked one piece in her pocket. She chewed the other half and opened her mouth. "Is my tongue black?"

Before Victor could answer, a familiar voice barked, "Dorothy Bolton, what in blazes are you doing here?" She looked up. Dad stood three feet away holding a bulging paper bag. He yanked her upright and marched her down the street. There was no time to say goodbye to Victor.

"Well, I..." started Dorothy, peeking at Dad's face. His thick eyebrows squeezed together in a solid line. His moustache jumped up and down as he kneaded his lips.

With every step, he huffed like a bull. Dorothy decided to wait.

Finally Dad asked in a low rumble, "Does your mother know where you are?"

"No," croaked Dorothy, "she thinks I'm at the church service."

"Sweet Lord, she'll be frantic. You must stop these wild escapades." Dad walked faster, half dragging Dorothy along the shoreline street to a wide concrete staircase beside their wharf.

Mam and Lydia spied them coming across the gangway. "Merciful Lord!" cried Mam. "I feared you had fallen overboard!" She clasped Dorothy tight and burst into tears.

"I'm afraid Dorothy snuck off the ship with that scamp, Victor," said Dad.

Mam pushed Dorothy out to arm's length. Dorothy hung her head, wishing she could throw herself overboard right now.

"Look at me, girl."

Dorothy reluctantly raised her head to meet Mam's blue eyes, glinting like cold steel.

"We'll settle with you later," Mam said sharply. "Lydia, take her to the cabin while we report she's safe." Dorothy felt Lydia's fingernails dig into her wrist as her sister trotted her down the deck.

They passed Mr. Thorpe and Rose, reading in the day room. Dorothy's face flamed when Mr. Thorpe looked up questioningly. Rose called, "Hi Dorothy. Do you want to see this book?"

"Dorothy may not stop now." Lydia dragged her to

the cabin and flung her on a bunk, now bare of covers. "Frank and Patrick and half the crew were searching for you."

"I...I'm sorry, Lydia. Victor promised we'd be back before church was finished."

"Well, you weren't," snapped Lydia. "It was a short service." Her lips quivered. "Then a lad said a girl in a green dress tried to sit on the railing and fell off. Everybody leaned over the railing looking for your body."

Dorothy stared at her sister.

Lydia dabbed her eyes with a hanky. "Don't you dare tell anyone I cried about you." She ransacked Mam's bag for the silver mirror and patted her face with Mam's powder puff. "Do I have your word of honour that you will stay put in this room?"

Dorothy nodded glumly.

"Good," said Lydia. "I have to help Mam tell all the concerned people that my sister is not dead, just a thoughtless moron who left ship without permission." After one last look in the mirror, Lydia hustled from the room.

Dorothy got up and peered forlornly through the porthole. She heard voices and thumping sounds. Flattening her face on the glass, she looked sideways. Workmen were still taking crates from the chutes, loading them onto carts and hauling them away.

She heard Mam's voice outside the door and strained to listen.

"...used to be well-mannered and obedient. What happened to her?"

"The journey has been stressful, Aggie. I blame

myself for uprooting the family." Dad's sad voice sparked a fire of shame in Dorothy's belly.

She slumped onto the bed, feeling that every drop of strength had been wrung from her. Like the wet laundry Mam used to feed through the clothes wringer while Lydia turned the crank. She wondered if the wringer was packed in one of their crates.

She heard Dad's voice. "I must find our baggage. Take her to Mr. Lloyd."

Mam opened the door.

Swallowing hard, Dorothy stood up.

"Your little adventure caused a frightful inconvenience for many people. The Reverend Mr. Lloyd wishes to speak to you." Mam marched Dorothy to the smoking saloon where Mr. Lloyd was packing his magazines.

"You had a terrible fright today, Mrs. Bolton," he said gently. "Go have tea. I'll fetch you when Dorothy is ready."

"Now, young lady!" Mr. Lloyd stared at Dorothy. "Today you broke two of our Lord's Commandments." His voice cut through her like a razor. "You broke the Fourth Commandment: Remember the Sabbath Day and Keep it Holy."

Dorothy's hand pressed against her mouth. What happened to people who broke the Lord's Commandments? Didn't they get turned to a pillar of salt?

"And the Fifth Commandment...what is the Fifth Commandment, Dorothy?"

"Hon...Honour thy Father and Mother," she stammered.

"Honour means obey, Dorothy." Mr. Lloyd's fierce eyes bored into Dorothy's head. "Will you obey them from now on?"

"Y...yes, Reverend Lloyd." Dorothy licked her finger; she wasn't turned to salt yet.

"The Lord will forgive you if you set things right with those you wronged." He pointed to a desk with writing materials laid out. "You shall write letters of apology."

"Yes, sir." Dorothy sank into the chair behind the desk, just in time. Her legs were shaking too hard to hold her upright.

"First, a letter to your mother, who suffered the most. Then a letter to the Head Steward, who released crew members to search for you. I shall judge whether or not your letters are satisfactory." Mr. Lloyd picked up his satchel of magazines and left the room.

A half hour later Dorothy's hand throbbed from gripping her pencil, but her letters were finished. She didn't dare move until Mr. Lloyd approved. Finally, he returned with Mam and scanned her work.

"Hmph," he said, "these will have to do. There are some spelling errors but you do not have time to correct them. I shall deliver your apology to the Head Steward, Dorothy. He is far too busy to see you."

Mr. Lloyd handed the other letter to Mam. "I believe Dorothy is genuinely repentant, Mrs. Bolton. Now it is time to forgive her and embrace the next step in our journey to the Promised Land."

"I am so indebted to you, Mr. Lloyd."

"Not at all, Mrs. Bolton. It is merely part of my duties as the Colony's chaplain."

"And lucky we are to have you. I'm sure Dorothy has learned her lesson."

Dorothy nodded. *I'll never listen to Victor again,* she promised herself. She felt ashamed for causing her family such distress. She thrust her hand in her pocket.

The piece of licorice was still there.

She rolled it in her fingers thinking, *but Victor is so much fun.*

13

April 12

Embarking On the Train

Hurry, Dodie," said Mam, "the family is waiting at the storage sheds." Dorothy hobbled out the door. Halfway down the hall Mam stopped. "Why are you limping?"

"My shoe fell off somewhere."

Mam squeezed her eyes shut. "Mercy," she groaned. "Well, you'll have to stumble along as best you can." They joined the throng descending the gangway.

Dorothy and Mam pushed through people searching the stacks of boxes and trunks. "Thank heaven Dad found our baggage earlier," said Mam. "He and Frank and Patrick piled it together."

"There's our Lydia, Mam!"

Lydia stood atop a trunk, waving her flowered hat. She climbed down to greet them. "The train stop is a quarter mile off. There are no porters or wagons, so Dad and Frank and Patrick have been carrying our crates. They look fearfully heavy."

Lydia pointed to a huddle of leather satchels. "Dad said one of you should stay here and the other can help bring the hand luggage."

"I can carry my own bag," Dorothy said hopefully.

Mam sighed. "Yes, that's best. Put your everyday boots on."

Dorothy rummaged through her bag. Sitting on the rough wooden dock, she laced up her sturdy boots and tucked her patent-leather shoe away.

Lydia picked up two satchels. "Let's go, Dodie."

As she climbed the concrete staircase, Dorothy's bag grew heavier and heavier. Seeing the determined grimace on Lydia's face, she choked back her complaint.

"Turn right here," puffed Lydia, at the top of the stairs. "At the next street, turn left. The train tracks cross that street."

Dorothy nodded, too short of breath to say anything.

When they reached the next turn Lydia asked, "Do you need a rest?"

Dorothy's arm throbbed. She shifted the case to her other hand. "Not if you don't."

"Well, I need a rest." At a storefront bench Lydia flopped down.

Dorothy dropped her bag, shook out her arm and sat beside her sister. "Lydia, does Mam approve of Patrick?"

Lydia looked at Dorothy cautiously. "She approves of the way he's helping us."

"Does she know Patrick wrote you a note?"

"No, she doesn't and don't you tell her!" Lydia stood in a huff and grabbed her bags. They trudged silently until they arrived where the railway tracks crossed the street. A hundred yards along the track they saw heaps of luggage on a platform.

"There they are!" cried Dorothy, pointing to three men sagged against a crate. Dorothy and Lydia lugged their satchels along the track. Patrick got up and met them, taking Lydia's cases. *What about me?* thought Dorothy indignantly, as she dragged her bag the rest of the way.

"Well, don't you have grit, Dodie-Podie," said Frank. That was the word Mr. Lloyd had used! It must be a compliment. Dorothy grinned.

"I'm glad you're here, Dodie," said Dad. "Guard this baggage while we go for another load." He ruffled her hair. "It's an important job." Dorothy's grin grew wider.

When the family left, Patrick reached for Lydia's hand. Dorothy exhaled a huff of irritation. What was so special about Lydia, anyway?

Perched on a crate, she wondered how Gram and Uncle Oliver were celebrating Easter. Gram probably cooked a goose with bread stuffing and roasted potatoes. Feeling lonely, Dorothy sucked her little stick of licorice.

Other immigrants trudged by with baggage. She saw Victor lugging a large box with his father and brother. They set it down nearby.

Victor rushed over to her. "Did you get in trouble, Dodie?"

Dorothy sighed. "I got a lecture from Reverend Lloyd about breaking the Ten Commandments. I missed tea and I'm starving. And I lost my Sunday-best shoe."

Victor slapped her playfully on the back. "I can solve those problems. I have the sweets *and* your shoe in my kit bag."

"You do?"

"Yes," said Victor with a grin. "I found it on the staircase."

"Did you get in trouble, Victor?"

Victor whistled. "I got quite a lecture from Curly about leaving ship without permission. Mom was cross but Pop didn't care. He said boys will be boys."

Victor's father called him. "I'll bring my kit bag on the next trip," he promised.

In the distance Dorothy heard church bells ringing. A middle-aged couple walked by, dressed in their Easter finery. The woman smiled at Dorothy. "Good evening, miss. Are you waiting for the immigrant train?"

"Yes," said Dorothy, "we're going to Sas...ka..." *What's the name of that town? Never mind.* "We're going to the North-West Territories."

"We wish you good fortune," said the man, tipping his hat. They walked briskly down the street toward the ringing bells.

When Dorothy's family returned she reported, "I met some Canadians. They were very friendly, but they had a strange accent."

"That's nice, pet," said Dad wearily, easing down his end of a large trunk. Frank dropped the other end and sat on it. Patrick and Lydia plunked down their box. They left for another load as soon as they caught their breath.

On Victor's next trip, he delivered the paper bag with her half of their purchase, plus one black shoe and a shiny red apple. Dorothy bit into the apple, thinking its crisp juicy flesh was the most delicious she had ever eaten.

After some dates and a Tootsie Roll, she tucked the bag into her travel case. Then she sat, tapping the crate with her feet. Finally her family turned the corner, hauling the final load of luggage. Lydia carried the basket of yapping puppies. With a squeal Dorothy jumped down.

"Don't open the basket," panted Lydia. "We can't chance losing the pups here."

Disappointed, Dorothy climbed on the crate again. Everyone else collapsed wherever they could.

"I am ready for bed," sighed Mam. "There had better be mattresses in the tourist cars as Mr. Barr promised."

Frank grimaced. "I don't put much faith in Barr's promises." Taking Mr. Barr's dog-eared letter from his leather bag, he searched for the section on trains.

"Here it is." Frank read aloud: *I have made a special arrangement...to have at least sufficient Tourist cars for all the women and children of the party...These cars are uphol-stered, and the beds are provided with mattresses, bedding, drop curtains, soap and towels in the lavatory.*

"I surely hope this promise is honoured," said Dad. "Which reminds me, we must take what we need and pack our soiled clothes away before the trunks get heaved into a baggage car."

"Fresh clothes," cried Mam and Lydia, jumping up.

After Dad unlocked the trunks, they carefully lifted layers of folded clothes. "A clean nightgown for you," said Mam, thrusting it in Dorothy's arms. "And a clean frock."

Lydia pulled out a white lace petticoat and blushed when she noticed Patrick watching her.

Good grief, thought Dorothy, *can't he ever stop staring at her?*

Dad aimed Patrick toward his luggage. "There won't be bedding in the colonist cars. You'd best unpack some rugs and soap and towels."

Frank lifted the lid of a trunk. Dorothy saw her lumpy

eiderdown on top. What were those bumps? Then she remembered.

"Wait, Frank!" She leapt to the trunk and carefully unrolled her quilt.

Frank whistled. "Mam will enjoy these, Dodie-Podie, but she'll have to wait for Saskatoon." He pulled out two blankets and two pillows, tucking the eiderdown back in the trunk.

Mam divided the food between two wicker baskets. "Bread, cheese, smoked sausage, apples, canned sardines, oatmeal, tea, milk and sugar. That should keep the wolf from the door for a couple of days." She packed bowls, cups and cutlery.

Dad brought pots to use on the cooking ranges that were guaranteed to be in every immigrant coach. "And most important of all," he said, producing two sturdy crockery teapots. "I hope the porters keep kettles on the boil as promised."

As night fell, people huddled under blankets and waited. Sitting on the crate with Dad, Dorothy cuddled inside his thick wool overcoat. "Halfway there, my pet," he whispered. "The iron rail will carry us the rest of the way." Dorothy closed her eyes, soothed by his steady heartbeat.

Suddenly she was startled awake. A monstrous black locomotive huffed past her, spewing steam from its underbelly and clanging a loud brass bell. Several coaches passed before the mighty engine wheezed to a stop. Dorothy swivelled her head, gaping at the long squealing beast.

"Frank, mind the baggage," yelled Dad. "Grab your

bags, ladies!"

Lugging her travel case stuffed with clean clothes, Dorothy joined a crowd jostling for position at the closest coach. Gold letters chiselled in the varnished wood announced: C.P.R. Tourist Car.

A uniformed porter stood by the door. He steadied Mam as she climbed into the coach and passed up her bag. The crowd pressed forward and Dorothy fell over her case. The porter blew a whistle, yelling, "Let's have order here! One at a time."

Dad lifted Dorothy to her feet and pushed her up the metal steps. He followed with her satchel and the wicker food basket.

"This car is reserved for women and children, sir," said the porter.

"I know," said Dad. "I'll just get them settled."

Mam walked halfway up the aisle and collapsed in a seat. Dorothy fell into the facing seat. Mam asked wearily, "Where's Lydia?"

Dad peered through the train window. "She's in the middle of the crowd." He opened the window and leaned out. "Mam's here, Lydia," he yelled with a wave.

Dorothy looked out the window. "Look, Dad, there's the Thorpes at the end of the queue. I'll save them a spot." She scrambled over her parents into the next compartment, stretching out on the maroon velour cushion.

From this position, Dorothy listened while arguing adults, cranky children and bawling babies settled into their new quarters. Finally the porter helped Mrs. Thorpe while Mr. Thorpe carried Rose, clasping her Cinderella doll.

"Aren't you sweet, Dorothy," said Mrs. Thorpe, wilting into the seat. "Your dad said you saved a place, so I didn't fret about being last." Dorothy cradled Rose who was too groggy to sit up. Mr. Thorpe helped the porter stow their luggage under the seat.

"I had best get beds prepared for all these tired children," said the porter. He unhooked wooden panels above each section. They fell open to make upper bunks fitted with mattresses and bedding.

Mam peered over the seat. "Dodie, go to the lavatory and then it's bedtime."

Dorothy lowered Rose's limp body to the seat and scrambled into the aisle. By the time she returned, the velour seats had been drawn out to make lower bunks.

"Take off your boots," said Mam, "then up you go." Dorothy climbed on the seat frame and squirmed into the bed suspended by brass chains from the sloping roof. Mam handed up her nightgown while Lydia pulled a blue curtain around their section.

Snug in her hanging nest, Dorothy listened to the clacking train wheels taking her to a new life somewhere in the wilderness of Canada.

14

The Iron Rail
Through Endless Forest

orothy awoke to the same sounds that had surounded her the night before: crying babies, cranky children, complaining adults. The blue curtain hid her from the rest of the crowded coach. She heard Rose whining for her dolly. Dorothy pulled her blankets over her head and fell back asleep.

When she woke again, the cozy blue cocoon was gone. Sunlight streamed across her face from the narrow ceiling window running the length of the train. Dorothy peered over the edge of her bunk.

Beneath her, the bed that Mam and Lydia shared had been restored to facing seats. Now there was a table between the seats with breakfast set out. Dorothy climbed down and stepped into the aisle, flicking frizzy hair off her face. She really needed to use the lavatory.

"Not so fast, young lady," said Mam, approaching with a steaming teapot. "Scrub your hands and face." She pointed to a folded hand towel on the table. "And bring the towel back. It has to last the whole trip."

The lavatory door was locked. Dorothy knocked and a familiar voice called, "Come back in five minutes, please."

Dorothy banged louder. "Hurry up, Lydia. I can't wait

that long."

Soon Lydia emerged with hairbrush and towel in hand. "You are such an annoying little wretch," she whispered as she passed. "Good morning, Mrs. Sutton," she said pleasantly to the woman behind Dorothy in line.

Dorothy jumped into the small bathroom and locked the door. She had to use the toilet too badly to offer an adult the next turn. *At least I don't take as long as Lydia,* she thought, hurriedly washing. She smiled at Mrs. Sutton as she left.

What was Victor's mother doing in their coach? Dorothy wondered where Mrs. Sutton was sitting and why she hadn't seen her last night. That thought faded as she wiggled into her seat where bread, cheese, dates and tea were waiting.

After breakfast Mam closed the curtain briefly while Dorothy dressed. Then Mam brushed her frizzy hair. Dorothy yelped every time the brush caught in a tangle.

"Mercy!" said Mam. "I don't think you brushed your hair at all aboard ship. I'll just have to smooth out the surface and secure it with a bow."

That's fine with me, thought Dorothy, staring at the dense forest rushing by.

"Is this the wilderness, Mam?"

"This is definitely a wilderness, Dodie, but not the one we're going to. I heard that the prairies have no trees at all."

Dorothy was trying to imagine a landscape bare of trees when a small body wiggled up beside her. "Ohhh," she groaned.

"I said you would entertain Rose this morning, Dodie, so her mother can rest."

Dorothy heard Reverend Lloyd's voice reminding her of yesterday's promise: *Obey your parents, Dorothy.* "Uh...certainly, Mam. May we use some paper?"

Dorothy decided to teach Rose to draw a person. "This circle is your head and this one is your body..."

Rose grabbed the pencil and stuck lines out of the head. Dorothy grunted in annoyance. She turned the paper over and made two new circles. She patted Rose's tummy. "Your legs start down here, under your belly."

"Let me try," squealed Rose. She finished Dorothy's drawing with legs coming out the bottom.

"And here's where your arms come out..."

After miles of trees had blurred past, Dorothy felt the train slowing. With a final huff it grated to a stop. "Look Rose, we're at a town beside a lake." Rose scrambled to the window and flattened her face against the glass. The station platform filled with passengers stretching their legs.

"Mam, everyone is walking around. May I take Rose outside?"

"I don't know," said Mam uncertainly. "I fear you'll be left behind or get back on the wrong coach."

"There's Daddy," squealed Rose. "He's coming to get me." Wiggling off the seat, she ran down the aisle. Dorothy ran after her. Mr. Thorpe climbed the steps into their car. Waving to Mam, he helped the girls down to the platform.

Dorothy saw Frank on a nearby bench. "I'll visit my brother, Mr. Thorpe. Don't worry, I'll get back on the right coach."

Frank smiled as Dorothy sat beside him. "Hi Dodie-Podie. How did you sleep?"

"Very comfortably," said Dorothy, "except I was

afraid of rolling down on Lydia every time the train went around a curve."

"You have a bed all to yourself? Lucky girl! Patrick and I are sharing an upper bunk, which surely isn't enough space for two big blokes like us."

"Why don't you sleep with Dad on the bottom, Frank? It's much wider."

"We thought to do that, but Mr. Thorpe got on our coach at the last minute. There weren't any empty compartments, so Dad offered to share our space."

Dorothy pointed to the diary on Frank's lap. "What are you writing?"

"I'm recording what I saw today. Do you want to hear?"

Dorothy nodded. "I didn't see much. Rose kept me so busy I couldn't look out the window."

Frank cleared his throat. *"Dense forests of fir and birch at each side of the track and here and there a clearing with a cluster of log cabins and a store or two. On the station platform is the total male population, and a motley crew they look –"*

"What does that mean?" asked Dorothy. "Motley crew?"

"Oh," said Frank, "it means a colourful mixture. Here's how I describe them." He found his place again and read: *"Yanks with red woolen shirts on and mostly lean muscular fellows. They all have their hands in their pockets and are busy spitting tobacco juice all over the place."*

"Why did you call the people 'Yanks'?"

"That's a nickname for an American. We took a shortcut through Maine."

Dorothy jumped up. "You mean I'm standing on American soil now?"

"Sorry, Dodie, we just crossed back into Canada." Frank nodded toward the small town. "This is Megantic, Quebec."

"Ohh," sighed Dorothy. "I missed the chance to see America." *Because of that annoying child, Rose,* she thought resentfully.

"I'll tell you a secret, Dodie-Podie. It's the same forest on both sides of the border."

Seeing Frank's grin, Dorothy couldn't help but giggle. Frank always raised her spirits. "Look," she said. "Lydia's opening the window." She tugged Frank toward the train.

"Mam wants to know what car you're in, Frank," yelled Lydia.

"We're in a colonist car, three coaches behind you." He waved to Mam sitting behind Lydia.

Above the buzz of the crowd, a deep voice yelled, "All aboard!" Mr. Thorpe hustled across the platform with Rose. Taking her hand, Dorothy helped her into the coach. As they walked down the aisle, the train lurched forward. Rose fell against Dorothy, who grabbed the back of a seat to keep from tumbling down.

"Mercy!" said Dorothy. "This is even worse than the ship."

Mrs. Thorpe reached for Rose. The train swayed sideways and Dorothy toppled into the compartment beside them. She noticed the folding table tucked against the wall. "Why isn't your table set up, Mrs. Thorpe?"

Mrs. Thorpe sighed, "In truth, Dorothy, my belly is too fat to fit under it."

"Why *is* your belly so fat, Mrs. Thorpe?"

As soon as the words slipped out Dorothy's face reddened. "I...I'm sorry," she stuttered. "It's just that I've worried about you. Are you...ill?"

Mrs. Thorpe laughed. "No, not ill at all. I've a bun in the oven." She placed her hands under her bulging tummy. "A really big one, by the feel of it."

"A bun in the oven?" echoed Dorothy. Squeezing her eyes shut she thought, *that doesn't make any sense.* "But," she blurted, "Lydia said you were in the family way."

"That's right, Dorothy. I'm making a family."

Dorothy felt Rose poking her side, but her attention was rivetted to Mrs. Thorpe.

Mrs. Thorpe patted her arm. "I'm growing a baby in my belly. It will be born soon."

Dorothy's head reeled as she fell back against the seat. Her mouth dropped open but no sound came out. Finally she croaked, "I didn't know you could grow babies. I thought the doctor brought them." She looked up and saw Mam peering over the seat.

"Mrs. Bolton, forgive me," said Mrs. Thorpe, "I didn't realize you hadn't told Dorothy the facts of life yet."

Mam sighed. "With all this humanity crushed together, she is learning many facts of life before I planned. Bring Rose over here, Dodie, and let Mrs. Thorpe rest."

With Rose at her side, Dorothy moved next door. She stared at Mam questioningly. Mam blushed. "That's right, Dodie. Women make babies inside them. I'll explain more when you're old enough." Mam turned to look out the window.

When you're old enough, when you're old enough,

Dorothy mimicked under her breath. *I am old enough now*, she fumed. Her head swirled with mental fragments she couldn't piece together. Finally, she sighed and tucked the puzzle into a corner of her mind.

For the rest of the day Dorothy read and drew with Rose. She felt like a teacher and wondered if Rose was just as bored as she used to be. Whenever she checked out the window, there were tall, dark trees, nothing but trees.

During the night the train passed through two major Canadian cities. Dorothy was asleep, so Montreal and Ottawa remained just names in her mind.

The train steamed on through forests, broken by occasional lakes and small towns. When they stopped for a half hour at Sudbury, even Mam descended the steps to get fresh air. This town was big enough to have a train station. Mam and Dorothy walked through it and stood on a dirt street lined with shops.

Many men, including Dad, dashed down the street for provisions. Dorothy watched wistfully, but didn't ask to accompany him. It was only two days since Dad had dragged her along the main street of Saint John.

"Do you think Saskatoon will be like this, Mam?"

Mam lifted her skirt off the dusty ground. "This is a bit primitive. I surely hope Saskatoon will have cobble-stone streets."

Men emerged from shops holding large paper bags. There was no sign of Dad. Soon the street was full of shoppers swarming toward the station. Still no Dad.

Mam started to pace. "What is keeping him?"

Dorothy remembered her own experience. "With so many people in the shops, there must be very long queues."

Lydia ran up to them, puffing. "I didn't know where you were. The conductor is yelling 'All aboard'."

"Tell him to hold the train." There was an edge of alarm in Mam's voice. "I'll stay here and watch for Dad."

Lydia looked stricken. "I...I can't be that bold, Mam."

"I'll go with you, Lydia," said Dorothy.

They wove around people in the station and threaded their way through the crowd on the platform. Finally they pushed up to the conductor.

"Beg pardon, sir," said Lydia blushing. "Uh..." She seemed tongue-tied.

"Our Dad isn't back from shopping yet," Dorothy blurted out. "Please hold the train."

The conductor looked from Lydia to Dorothy. "Don't worry, young misses. We won't leave until everyone is aboard. Get on your coach now."

"Thank you," breathed Dorothy in relief.

"You're brave at speaking up, Dodie," said Lydia as they boarded.

"I learned to do that when everyone was ill on the ship." Dorothy sank into her seat, beaming at Lydia's approval.

Finally Mam boarded. "Dad, bless him, bought us fresh bread and milk and some homemade fruit preserves. Let's have tea."

The town of Sudbury disappeared in a flash and they sped through the endless forest of northern Ontario. That night Dorothy went to bed with the sweet taste of wild blueberries tingling on her tongue.

15

The Iron Rail
A Proper City

Early next morning, Dorothy scrambled down from her bunk. The table was set up but Mam and Lydia weren't there. Pushing up the window, Dorothy stuck her head out. Tall dark evergreens flashed by, just like yesterday. "Mercy," she exclaimed, "won't we ever get there?"

A throaty laugh rippled from the next compartment and a slight woman with a cheery smile peered over the seat. *Victor's mother, Mrs. Sutton!* Dorothy had never actually spoken to her. "Feeling a tad restless are you, honey?"

Before Dorothy could answer, Mrs. Sutton said, "Morning, Mrs. Bolton," and sank out of sight.

After a curt nod to Mrs. Sutton, Mam addressed Dorothy. "Good gracious, close that window. Can't you see the gritty smoke blowing in?" Mam set a pot of tea on the table. "Look at your dirty face! Go clean up before breakfast."

At the lavatory, Dorothy studied her face in the mirror. There were some cinder speckles on her cheeks, but not enough to fuss over. She had only stretched her head out the window for one minute.

When she returned she noticed that Mrs. Sutton was

no longer sitting in Mrs. Thorpe's compartment. Why had she been there?

"Dorothy," chirped Rose, "your mum says you'll play with me after breakfast."

"How nice," said Dorothy in a flat voice.

While Lydia set out bread and cheese, Mam poured tea into metal mugs. "Rose will sit with us so her mother can rest. I'm sure you won't mind entertaining her again."

Why not, thought Dorothy, *there's nothing interesting to see out the window*. Rose insisted on drawing Canadian trees, long lines with triangles zigzagging down the trunks. Trees on the drawing paper, trees outside. Dorothy was so weary of evergreens.

Suddenly people exclaimed in surprise and rushed to the windows on the far side of the coach. Dorothy and Rose squeezed up against Bertha and Madeline, two children in the opposite compartment.

Over Bertha's head Dorothy saw what had caused the collective gasps: a broad expanse of water stretched to the horizon. Were they back at the ocean again?

"Lake Superior," called the porter.

All day the train hugged the twisting shoreline, offering a welcome change of scenery. Even more delightful, in Dorothy's opinion, was the snaking track that sent people lurching every time the train whistled around a bend.

And on top of that, there were clumps of dirty white snow under the trees. Imagine, snow in April! Dorothy thought they were rocks until the porter explained.

In late afternoon the train huffed to a stop at Fort

William and the porter announced a one-hour break. Dorothy noticed Victor walking a dog on a leash. In her sweetest voice she asked, "May I go outside for fresh air, Mam?"

"I'll come with you," said Mam, lifting her hat and coat from the hook. Dorothy sighed as Victor strolled along the platform and out of sight.

"I must speak to Dad about replenishing provisions," said Mam.

"May I go with him?" asked Dorothy, pulling on her coat. "He'll need help to carry things." She followed Mam down the aisle, waiting for an answer.

At the door Mam stopped and surveyed the crowd. "Willy," she called, "take Dodie with you to the shop!" She looked at Dorothy. "Mind you act like a lady."

Dorothy nodded, trying to stop her feet from dancing.

She came back bubbling with news about the large Hudson's Bay Company Store. "You should have seen it, Mam. Big stacks of cloth in different colours. And barrels of dried beans and leather things hanging on the wall for horses –"

Dad laughed. "I hope we have such a well stocked shop in Saskatoon."

"– and Dad bought me a pad of paper and a new pencil. AND THIS!" She held up a small rectangular object with a cone-shaped hole.

Mam turned the small shape over in her hand. "What on earth is it?"

"A pencil sharpener!" said Dorothy excitedly. "It's a new invention from America. Now Dad won't have to whittle the pencil with a pocket knife."

Humming cheerfully, Dorothy boarded the train. Mam followed with a pound of corned beef, a slab of cheese and two loaves of fresh, warm bread.

In early evening, the train pulled to a stop in the middle of nowhere. There wasn't even a station, just a short platform surrounded by trees and rocks. Dorothy stared out the window, watching the trees darken to jagged black spikes against a purple sky. The forest looked frightfully spooky at night.

Finally Mam called the porter. "Why are we waiting, sir?"

"There's only a single rail, Madam, and the scheduled train has first claim. We must wait at the siding until the train from the west passes. It might be several hours."

"May we take some air on the platform?" asked Lydia.

"No, miss, the conductor won't let anyone out. There are bears about."

"Bears?" echoed Dorothy, remembering Tony's threat. "Will they hurt you?"

"Generally, no. But they are wild animals and unpredictable."

"Better safe than sorry," agreed Mam.

Rose stood on her seat, listening wide-eyed to this conversation. "The Three Bears didn't hurt Golden Hair," she reported.

The porter laughed. "Do you have the story of The Three Bears, little miss?"

"Right here," she said, holding up *Aunt Friendly's Nursery Book*.

Mrs. Thorpe asked the porter to make their bed so she could settle Rose for the night. Dorothy watched him swing an iron bar out from the base of a seat and attach it to the base of the facing seat. Then he tugged the seats together. The seat backs dropped into a mattress resting on the iron bar.

The porter unhooked the upper bunk and retrieved the bedding stored there during the day. With a snap, he spread sheets over the mattress.

"There, Miss Golden Hair. Much more comfortable than the beds in the Three Bears' house." Chuckling, the porter moved on.

Rose looked at Dorothy. "Will you read me the story, Dodie?"

"Oh, please do," said Mrs. Thorpe. "I'd like to have a wash in the lavatory."

Dorothy perched on the edge of the bed and Rose curled against her. She just finished reading when Mrs. Sutton walked down the aisle. Sitting next to them, she explained, "I sleep on the bunk above."

"Where do you go all day?" asked Dorothy. She shifted away from Rose who was starting to fidget.

"I walk through the coaches to the car where my men are."

"Oh!" said Dorothy. *I didn't know people could walk through the train to visit other people*, she thought. She squirmed as Rose grasped her shoulders.

"I have something for you." Mrs. Sutton passed Dorothy a note.

Surprised, Dorothy unfolded it.

> *Dodie, I am still looking after the dog. At the end of the trip the man will pay me another quarter. What kind of sweets do you fancy?*

Dorothy reached into her pocket for her freshly sharpened new pencil. Resting the note on Rose's storybook, she wrote back:

> When we get to Saskatune let's look in the store together. I hope they have lots of choise.

She felt Rose's arms curl around her neck.

"Thank you for being Victor's friend, Dodie," said Mrs. Sutton. "He needs a nice friend like you. It will help to settle him down."

Why does Victor have to settle down? thought Dorothy. *I like him just as he is.* Rose's cheek pressed against hers as she finished her reply: *I like being your friend.*

Dorothy handed the note back to Mrs. Sutton and ruffled Rose's hair. *I like being your friend too,* she thought with surprise.

That night Dorothy fell asleep wondering about Victor's family. It felt strange knowing his mother lay just beyond her reach. If she poked through the curtain at the end of her bunk, she would touch Mrs. Sutton's head.

When Dorothy awoke, the coach was abuzz with voices. But one sound was missing, the clackety-clack of the wheels humming along the track. *Don't tell me we're still at that siding,* she moaned. She peered over her bunk into the blue-tinted light below. Sitting in her petticoat, Lydia shook out a green wool shirt.

"What's happening, Lydia?"

Lydia looked up scowling. "It's confounded impossible to keep clothes neat in this wretched little compartment."

"I mean, where are we?"

"We're at Winnipeg and we're going to be here for hours. Many people have already got off so Mam thought there might be space at the stove to cook porridge." Lydia took Dorothy's dress from the hook and passed it up. "Hurry and get dressed."

Dorothy wiggled out of her nightgown. *Winnipeg!* she thought excitedly, *That's the place Frank mentioned, where all the blokes are getting off who aren't ready to be farmers.* When she was dressed, Lydia opened the curtain and called the porter to set up their table. The coach was half empty, and the remaining people were pulling on coats.

Mam returned with a steaming pot of oatmeal. "Finally a hot breakfast," she announced, quite pleased with herself. "These vittles should stick to your stomach."

As she ate, Dorothy stared out the window restlessly. Outside, people milled about on a platform in front of a wide brick building. It was three stories high with dormer windows on top. "Look how grand this station is, Mam. Shall we get off to look around?"

"I expect Dad will come for us soon." After finishing her oatmeal, Mam glanced out the window. "This is the most impressive station we've seen since Ottawa. Winnipeg must be an important city." Mam's voice got an excited ring. "I must groom properly!" She pulled her bag from beneath the seat and fled to the lavatory.

Dorothy pressed her face against the glass, scanning the crowd. Finally she exclaimed, "Look, Lydia! There's Dad standing under the porch roof, at the station door." She grabbed her coat and tam and ran down the aisle, ignoring Lydia's command to wait. She jumped down to the platform and wove her way through the crowd.

When she reached Dad she asked, "Shall we get to see Winnipeg?"

"Absolutely, my kitten. We'll be here for eight hours."

"Mam wants to see Winnipeg, too." Dorothy grabbed Dad's hand and tugged him toward her coach.

Dad waved to Mam and Lydia, who were descending the steps with their skirts lifted carefully. "What a sturdy structure this is, bigger than the station at York," he said, gesturing toward the building. "Come see inside, it's very comfortable."

As they walked through the large waiting room, Dorothy gaped at the polished oak benches and the marble floor.

"What a relief to walk on smooth marble," said Mam, "instead of rough wooden boards."

"I got information about Winnipeg from the station clerk," said Dad, unfolding a paper. Following his hand-drawn map, they boarded an electric street car and headed along Main Street to the downtown shopping district.

"The clerk described how fast Winnipeg has grown in the last few years," said Dad. "There's about fifty thousand people living here. That's almost as big as York."

Dorothy stared out the window. Winnipeg didn't look anything like York. The street was so wide and the buildings were so new. "Look how tall that building is, Dad."

Dad held his finger out to count the levels. "Six stories," he said. "The clerk told me they are building a new bank that will be ten stories high. Imagine that!"

They had dinner in a hotel dining room with electric chandeliers hanging from the ceiling. A proper English dinner of roast beef and Yorkshire pudding!

"How lovely Winnipeg is," exclaimed Mam. "I shall enjoy living in Canada if Saskatoon is a proper city like this."

Dorothy watched Dad's grin fade as he turned his face away.

He knows something he isn't telling us, she thought.

16

The Iron Rail

Not Again!

After Winnipeg, the rocks and trees disappeared and the landscape collapsed to a flat expanse of grey grass. The dull land droned on, relieved only by a brief stop at Brandon for water and coal. The train didn't even lurch around corners now; it just went on and on in a straight line.

This is worse than the forest, thought Dorothy. *Lydia was right, there's nothing here.* She was so bored, she even wished she were back in Miss Davis's classroom.

At suppertime Mam took the teapot to line up for hot water.

Dorothy stood in the aisle to stretch her legs. The train wasn't swaying at all; it was easy to keep her balance. Suddenly she had an idea. "Rose, Bertha and Madeline, do you want to play follow-the-leader?" The girls scrambled off their seats and lined up behind her.

Dorothy hopped down the aisle, left knee up, right boot clicking the floor. The three children copied like shadows. "Now switch!" Obediently they bounced their left feet down, right knees up under their dark serge dresses. "Clear the way," she ordered a pair of grimy boys who scooted between two seats.

At the end of the aisle, a group of women huddled around the small stove. Mam turned. One hand held her teapot; the other clasped a steaming kettle.

"Don't you have any sense?" she hissed. "Not down here!"

Dorothy jolted to a stop. Climbing on an empty seat, she swung her laced boot over the back of the next one. That section was occupied. "Oops, sorry," she said to a severe-looking woman reading a newspaper. "Just passing through." She lugged each child over the seat, ignoring the woman's muttering about uncivilized behavior.

"Follow the leader," Dorothy called, racing up the aisle.

"For Pete's sake, Dodie," yelled Lydia, "sit down and act like a lady!"

Dorothy stuck out her tongue. Lydia returned a dis-approving glare, smoothed her skirt and resumed reading her book.

Dorothy hopped on both feet. Rose, Bertha and Madeline giggled as they copied her. Suddenly the train's whistle blasted, wheels screeched and the four girls tumbled backwards onto the gritty floor.

"Not again," the adults in the car moaned collectively. "Not another delay!"

Dorothy brushed off the girls and sent them to their seats. She scrambled across Lydia's lap and opened the window. Leaning out she cried, "Heavens! There's hundreds of beautiful animals crossing the track. What are they?"

"Get off my skirt, Dodie. You left a dirty footprint." Lydia nudged her and squeezed out the window for a look. "I don't know, but it's a bloomin' big herd. We'll be stuck here forever."

Lydia's comment was punctuated by the sound of gunfire. From the cars behind them, men poured out. They swarmed over the scruffy grassland aiming shotguns and pistols toward the vast herd.

Dorothy waved. "Hi, Dad!" She pulled her head inside the train and grabbed her coat. "I'm going outside." Ignoring Lydia's protests, she ran down the aisle to the steps. The outside door was latched and the porter wasn't nearby to open it.

Dorothy remembered what Mrs. Sutton had said about going through the coaches. Past the lavatory was another door. She tried it and found herself on an open platform between cars. Unlatching the half door in the railing, she jumped to the ground. Dry grass crunched under her feet as she ran across the prairie.

Dad looked surprised when she grabbed his hand. "You shouldn't be 'ere, Dodie. These fools are trigger 'appy."

"Will they kill those beautiful animals, Dad?"

Dad called to the nearest hunter, "Jack, boy, don't waste your bullets. You can't take an antelope aboard anyway!"

Jack waved his Stetson hat in reply. "Blimey! Ain't never seen a sight like this!" He fired off another round with his shiny new revolver.

"You couldn't 'it a target if it was right before you," yelled Dad. He grinned at Dorothy. "These gentlemen ain't never 'ad guns in their 'ands before. They went crazy shopping for western gear at Winnipeg."

Dorothy grinned back. She knew Dad was excited; he was talking fast and dropping his h's.

Then his voice turned serious. "Get back on the train, Dodie, before one of these blasted fools shoots you."

Before Dorothy could protest, a loud voice thundered across the prairie. "Put those guns down!" The train's conductor walked forward, yelling through a megaphone.

"Immediately!" he emphasized, "or you will not be permitted to reboard."

Kicking at clumps of grass, the men lowered their guns.

"Nobody wants to be left behind on the bald prairie," said Dad.

Dorothy surveyed the sea of grass. "I should think not," she said indignantly. "There's nothing here."

"There must be over a thousand antelope in that herd," said Dad with wonder in his voice. Dorothy leaned against him until the graceful tawny and white animals disappeared across the tracks.

As they walked toward her coach, Dorothy held Dad's hand. He pointed to a little brown animal darting into a burrow. "Never doubt that there's something here, Dodie. We just have to find it."

Dorothy looked across the land. There were many little animals scampering over the ground and diving into holes. Dad was right as always. She thought about this strange prairie that was already revealing its secrets.

"Will our homestead look like this, Daddy?"

"Better. Art Sutton told me our colony is in an especially fertile zone with rivers and wooded areas."

"But Dad, you had a strange look when Mam said she thought she would enjoy Canada." Dorothy stared into his eyes. "Remember, at the hotel in Winnipeg."

Dad shifted uncomfortably. "I heard some rumours about Saskatoon," he sighed. "I fear your Mam will be mightily disappointed in that town."

Dad's confession was interrupted by the call, "All aboard!" The porter from Dorothy's coach rushed out and whisked her up the steps. Dad sprinted toward his car.

When Dorothy sat down Mam said, "Gracious, Dodie, you set my heart racing. Running amok with all those lunatics. Won't you ever learn to act like a lady?"

"Just a minute, please." Dorothy leaned out the window and watched Dad jump up his steps just as the train shunted forward. She pulled the window shut and smiled at Mam. "So the smoke doesn't ruin our supper," she said.

"Quite so," said Mam. "The tea is over-steeped now but I'll thin yours with extra milk." As she prepared Dorothy's tea she added, "The porter said we shall be in Saskatoon tomorrow." Mam got a wistful look. "I hope we can procure a comfortable hotel room with a hot bath."

Dorothy nodded slowly. She tried to eat a bologna sandwich but her stomach churned. She was sure Saskatoon would not have the fancy hotel Mam was imagining.

In the morning the train stopped in Regina, right beside another train. Dorothy opened the window and stretched out. She could almost touch a cow peering at her through the open slats of a cattle car. The bellows of complaining cattle and the stench of manure blasted into their compartment.

Mam yanked her inside and closed the window.

"Settlers' stock," explained the porter.

"What do you mean?" asked Lydia.

"Americans moving here for the free land and bringing their livestock with them."

"Goodness," said Mam, "I hope they won't settle anywhere near us."

"You would do well to settle near them, Madam," said the porter. "They're experienced farmers."

"Humph," said Mam when the porter moved on. "Mr. Barr promised there wouldn't be any upstart Americans near us."

"Why don't you like Americans, Mam?" asked Dorothy.

"The British Empire wasn't good enough for them." Mam's huffy tone ended the discussion.

After Regina the train bumped along slowly. The track felt rougher now.

"More barren prairie," sighed Mam.

"Not quite barren," noted Dorothy. "I saw ponds full of wild birds. They flew up when the train went past. Here's a pond now!" She laughed while a flock of large birds ran awkwardly across the water with long black necks stretched forward. Finally, flapping wings lifted their heavy bodies into the air.

Lydia leaned against the window to look. "I've seen drawings of those birds," she said. "They're Canada geese. They're supposed to be very tasty."

"Oh, Mam," said Dorothy, "when Frank buys a gun he can shoot us some!"

Mam's face pinched even tighter than usual. She excused herself and went to the lavatory.

"Don't talk like that, Dodo!" sputtered Lydia.

"Why not?" said Dorothy, "Dad said there's no gamekeepers here."

"Can't you see Mam is worried about Frank getting hurt?"

"Oh," said Dorothy. She closed her eyes and tried to see their journey through her mother's eyes. Every meal, Mam stood in line by the stove to bring hot tea back to their table. She kept track of their food and their clothes. She hung up Dorothy's dress every night so the wrinkles would fall out.

When Mam returned, Dorothy reached over and squeezed her hand. "Thanks for taking care of us, Mam...and worrying about us." Mam squeezed back and her eyes glistened for a second before she turned to the window.

Dorothy's stomach clenched into a knot, thinking about the disappointment awaiting Mam only a few hours away.

17

April 17, 1903

The End of the Journey by Steam

In early evening the conductor walked by calling, "End of the line. Saskatoon."

Dorothy peered out her window. The train clattered across a long wooden bridge spanning the banks of a wide river. The river was full of large whitish-grey chunks. Dorothy stared down. Was that ice?

Mam tucked the remnants of teatime into the wicker case. Dorothy and Lydia shoved stray articles into their travel bags. The car buzzed with excitement. Finally the train huffed to a stop beside a long platform.

Through the window Dorothy surveyed the immense, mauve-tinted sky. Beneath the sky a few small wooden structures sat in a field. *Where is the town?* she thought in alarm. She craned her neck to look through the window across the aisle. On that side of the train, row after row of cone-shaped white tents covered the ground.

Suddenly the aisle was crammed with colonists eager to squeeze out the door. Dorothy, Mam and Lydia thrust on their coats and hats and joined the line. Dorothy was bursting with curiousity. Then she noticed Mrs. Thorpe sagging heavily in her seat. Beside her, Rose clung forlornly to her doll.

Dorothy squeezed her eyes shut and decided what she had to do. She tugged Mam's coat. "I'll stay and look after Rose." She took off her coat and hat and dropped into the empty seat opposite Mrs. Thorpe.

"I can't face that crowd, Dorothy." Mrs. Thorpe's face contorted. "I've such a backache."

"Shall you lie down, Mrs. Thorpe?" Dorothy asked anxiously. "I know how to make the bed." Mrs. Thorpe nodded.

"Sit in our section for a minute," Dorothy said. She helped Mrs. Thorpe waddle to the next seat. "You too, Rose, and bring Cinderella."

Dorothy dropped on hands and knees to examine the bar beneath the seat. She unhooked it and pulled it across to the other bench as she had watched the porter do. She tugged on the seat. It didn't budge. She tugged harder, pulling upwards. The velour cushion sprang forward, tumbling Dorothy into the opposite seat.

"Halfway there," she announced triumphantly.

"Goodness, child, what are you doing?" It was the porter.

"Mrs. Thorpe needs to rest."

The porter took in the situation and finished preparing the bed. "The folks on the platform will be back for the night as well."

"Really?" asked Dorothy.

He nodded toward the far window. "Those tents are full and the rest won't be unloaded until tomorrow."

Cheers erupted from the crowd on the platform. "The Colonization Agent finally finished his welcome speech," explained the porter. The crowd dispersed but nobody came inside.

Dorothy helped Mrs. Thorpe into bed, then she read to Rose. Digging through the basket, she found crackers and cheese for bedtime snack. She took Rose to the bathroom. Finally she tucked Rose and Cinderella in bed beside Mrs. Thorpe and closed their curtain.

With the passengers gone, the coach was eerily quiet. Dorothy sat in an empty compartment so she could study those tents again. Flattening her face against the train window, she saw silhouettes of people sitting around campfires. Farther back, the glow of other campfires cast strange shadows on the canvas tents. It looked spooky.

She moved back to her own seat. For a long time she watched dim shapes milling about outside. Twilight had darkened into night by the time Mam and Lydia returned. Mam sat heavily. "This is worse than Hades," she groaned. "Why did I ever agree to come here?" She leaned her elbows on the table and buried her head in her hands.

Dorothy's heart pounded. Never before in her life had she heard Mam utter a profanity. Finally she breathed, "What's wrong?" Mam didn't answer.

Lydia fumed, "This paltry excuse of a town isn't even big enough for a village. The road is a muddy rut. There's one miserable boardwalk that connects two pubs."

"Mercy!" said Dorothy. She hardly dared ask, "Is... is there a hotel?"

"The pubs have rooms on the second floor, but they're full."

"Oh, my," said Dorothy.

She and Lydia looked at each other for a long minute.

Then Dorothy said, "I shall make Mam some tea." She ransacked the wicker case for the teapot and spooned tea leaves into it. Then she pushed past returning passengers to the stove where a full kettle was simmering. The porter filled her teapot and Dorothy brought it carefully to the table.

Lydia set out the metal cups and the bit of milk left in the bottle they had purchased in Winnipeg. Was it only yesterday they had eaten dinner in a dining room in that grand city? Mam sipped her tea silently, then dropped her head into her hands again.

"Let's make up the bed, Lydia. I know how." While Mam sat across the aisle they attached the bar, tugged the cushions and tucked the sheets into place.

Lydia pulled the blue curtain. Mam let Lydia undress her while Dorothy went to the lavatory to wet a wash-cloth for Mam's face. Then Dorothy put on her night-gown and climbed to her hanging bunk.

She lay in bed listening to people shuffling in the aisles, settling restless children and venting frustration. She wanted a hug from Dad, but it was too dark to look for him. She would have to wait until morning. Things were always better in the bright light of morning, Gram used to say. Come to think of it, Mam often said that too.

The next day, brilliant sunshine filled the car. Dad knocked on the window and invited them to the so-called hotel for breakfast. "Come on, Aggie," he coaxed. "I've checked the menu. A hearty meal of bacon and eggs will do wonders for your spirits."

The meal did wonders for Dorothy's spirits, anyway. While Mam returned to the railway coach, she and Lydia went with Dad to purchase two bell tents from the freshly unloaded stack. They helped Frank and Patrick drag the large canvas bags over the scruffy ground, past five hundred assembled tents, to the edge of the open prairie.

"Where shall we pitch our new home, Dodie?" asked Dad.

Brown grass and silver-grey bushes extended flatly to the western horizon. Dorothy laughed and threw her arms in the air. "Anywhere!"

"How about right here?" said Lydia.

Frank and Patrick dropped the bags.

"Oh, I forgot one thing," said Dad. He took Frank and Patrick aside and pointed down the field. They nodded and dragged one bag fifty yards away.

Dad dumped the remaining bag. "You'll have to help me figure this out, ladies." He examined the canvas and picked up the ropes and pegs. Then he scratched his chin. "We don't have a centre pole. There must be a separate pile on the platform." Dad strode back through the confusion of tents toward the train.

"What's that about?" Dorothy pointed to Frank and Patrick sorting out their tent across the field.

"Mam doesn't want Patrick near me," said Lydia, kicking the roll of canvas that would be their new home. "Last night he asked if he could court me and Mam said I was too young." Lydia sat on the canvas, tears rolling down her face.

Dorothy fumbled in her pocket, pulled out a slightly dirty handkerchief and dabbed Lydia's cheeks. "Mam is just...sad, right now. Patrick should ask again later."

"She said he can ask when he proves up his homestead."

"What does that mean?"

"He has to build a house and plow some acres. I forget how many. He has three years to do it and then he gets clear title of his land."

Dorothy's brain ached from trying to think of some way to comfort Lydia. "But Lydia, Patrick is going to live with our Frank. You'll see him every time you visit Frank." She could hardly believe what she had just said. Only a few days ago she had been jealous of Patrick's interest in Lydia. Now she wanted Lydia to be happy.

"You can...uh, bake bread and take it over."

Lydia stopped sniffling and smiled. "You've got a good heart, Dodie."

By the time Dad returned with a six-foot wooden pole, Dorothy and Lydia had the canvas spread in a circle with guy ropes and pegs laid in place. Dad slid the pole through the door and wiggled it until he found the point of the roof. He pushed the pole upright and the canvas dangled over it like a limp ghost.

"Dodie, hold the pole while we nail down the pegs."

Dorothy slipped under the heavy, musty canvas. The pole swayed as Dad and Lydia tugged the edges, but finally the sloping roof spread into a taut cone with short walls around the bottom. The roof glowed golden in the sunlight.

Through the sunlit canvas Dorothy watched Lydia's silhouette stand and arch her back. "I've never done anything like that before," Lydia said proudly.

"Me neither," said Dad.

Dorothy flipped open the door flap. "Our new prairie home!"

Dad laughed. "It looks very cozy."

"Oh, I almost forgot," he added. "Mr. Thorpe's back at the train platform. He can't get anything done with Rose hanging on him. I told him we'd help." They found Mr. Thorpe sitting on a crate, dandling Rose and her doll on his knee.

"Come, Rose," said Dorothy. "Let's take Cinderella for a walk round town."

"Wait, Dodie," said Dad. "How will you find your way back to our tent?"

Dorothy studied the tents that surrounded her like hundreds of pointed icebergs. "Uh…we'll come back to the train, Dad, and sit with Mrs. Thorpe."

Dorothy grasped Rose's hand. They walked to a huddle of wooden buildings, the tan colour of freshly sawn wood. Two taller buildings stood at each end of a plank sidewalk with little shops between them. Beyond the last building, men examined some green and red wagons.

Dorothy lifted Rose to look in the first shop window. There were shovels and ropes and lanterns hanging on the wall.

"Dodie!"

Dorothy jumped and turned around. Victor stood on the boardwalk, holding a large metal washtub.

"I looked for you every time the train stopped," he said.

"I saw you once, walking a dog, but Mam wanted me to stay with her."

Victor reached in his pocket. "The gentleman paid me another quarter. Let's buy some sweets right now."

Dorothy looked doubtful. "Do they sell sweets here?"

"Yes, at Cairn's Confectionery and Bakery."

Dorothy pointed beside her. "We'll have to share with Rose." Rose beamed her most winsome smile in Victor's direction.

"Surely," said Victor. "I can buy lots of treats with a quarter." He led them to the shop and set the washtub upside down on the boardwalk. "You two sit on this; I'll be back in a minute."

Dorothy perched beside Rose and watched people pass by. She recognized some of them from the ship. Then she inhaled the delicious smell of fresh baking.

"Oatmeal raisin biscuits," said Victor, holding out two warm cookies.

"My grandma made biscuits like this," said Rose.

"Mine too," said Dorothy, feeling a flush of sadness.

"Wanna know why we just bought this tub?" asked Victor as he munched his cookie. Dorothy nodded.

"The chap next to us gashed his leg chopping wood; there was blood everywhere. So Pop got the idea of standing in a tub." Dorothy gave him a puzzled look. "In case we miss the log," he explained, "when we swing the axe."

Dorothy squeezed her eyes shut to blot out the image of a mangled leg. *Dear Lord,* she prayed, *don't let Dad and Frank chop their legs off. Or Patrick,* she added, remembering that he might join the family.

18

Saskatoon
A New Life

When Dorothy and Rose returned to the train, Mrs. Thorpe was gone. The only passenger still aboard was Mam, wilted listlessly against her seat.

"Excuse me, miss," said the porter. "Your mother must get off now. The train will be leaving soon."

Dorothy stared at the porter, then at Mam.

"Your sister took the luggage a while ago, but she couldn't persuade your mother to move."

Dorothy stood there uncertainly. Rose leaned into her, sucking her thumb.

"I've seen this before," said the porter sympathetically. "For some people the shock is too great when they first see the wilderness. She'll feel better when she gets settled and unpacks the pretty things she brought from England."

Now Dorothy knew what to do. "Come Mam," she said brightly. "I have something special for you at the tent."

A glimmer of interest crossed Mam's face. "What is it?"

"A surprise."

Dorothy hoped desperately that the lumps inside her eiderdown had not broken. Extending her hand, she coaxed Mam along the aisle, with Rose hanging on her other arm. The porter helped them down to the platform.

He patted Dorothy on the back. "You'll do well in the wilderness, miss. You've got grit."

Dorothy looked at him, puzzled. Then she remembered Reverend Lloyd's speech and smiled. "That's because I'm British, sir."

She led Mam and Rose through the labyrinth of tents. *Keep walking until we reach the open land*, she told herself. But more tents had gone up and there was no longer a clear trail. They manoeuvered between guy ropes until they finally reached the edge of the encampment.

By this time Mam was moaning about the end of civilization and Rose was whining for her daddy. All the tents looked the same and Dorothy couldn't see anybody familiar. For a minute she panicked. Then she noticed Frank and Patrick walking the pups out in the field.

"FRANK!" she yelled, "I CAN'T FIND OUR TENT!"

Loping across the dry grass, Frank took Mam's arm and guided them. "Isn't it a beautiful sunny day, Mam? I was at your tent a while ago. Dad and Lydia are making it comfortable." Dad had opened one of the crates and set Mam's rocking chair in front of the tent. Frank eased her into it.

Dorothy exclaimed at the sight of a small tin stove sitting on the ground with a steaming kettle atop.

"Dad just bought it," explained Lydia, "and your friend, Victor, brought some chopped wood and showed us how to light it. I'll brew tea now and we'll eat the rest of the food in the wicker basket."

"Lydia, where's the trunk with our bedding?"

"In the tent. Dad unlocked it but I haven't had time to get anything out."

Dorothy rushed into the tent. Soon she came out cradling something cool and smooth in her hand.

"Dodie, get a cup for Mam from the basket."

"I have something better!" Dorothy held up her treasure.

Lydia blinked. "Where did that come from?"

"It was wrapped in my eiderdown and it didn't break!"

Dorothy served Mam's tea in a porcelain cup and saucer, delicately painted with blue castles. Mam held the teacup while tears rolled down her face. She sipped slowly, rocking back and forth on the crunchy grass.

Dorothy stood beside her anxiously.

Finally Mam set the teacup on the grass and searched Dorothy's face. Mam's eyes had a strange, questioning look. Dorothy waited nervously for a rebuke.

Finally Mam said, "I was wrong about you, Dodie." She squeezed Dorothy's hand. "You really are a lady. Inside, where it counts the most."

Dorothy's tension evaporated. Her spirit felt light enough to soar into the immense blue sky.

Later she took Mam to the store where they bought potatoes, onions and dried beef. While a savory stew simmered on the stove, Dorothy went next door to the Thorpe's tent to invite them for supper.

After sunset Patrick and Frank arrived with an armload of firewood. Dorothy noted with relief that there were no axe marks on their legs. She helped pull grass to clear a circle of bare ground. Later they all sat around a crackling hot campfire.

"Heavens, it's getting cold," said Mrs. Thorpe, tugging at her coat which didn't nearly cover her wide belly. "Rose and I should retire."

Rose started wailing. "My dolly, I can't go to bed without my dolly!"

"Did you leave it on the train?" asked Dorothy. "No, you had it when we walked to the shops. You must have dropped it when you ate the biscuit."

"Rose, stop crying," said Mr. Thorpe. "It's too dark to get it now. We'll find it tomorrow."

Dorothy hugged her. "I'll look in the morning. Be a big girl now and help your mummy go to sleep." Still sniffling, Rose walked between her parents to their tent, twenty feet away.

Dorothy pulled her coat collar tighter around her neck. "I'm cold, Dad."

"You'll be warm in bed, my pet. Lydia and I stuffed your mattress with straw. Keep your outside clothes on and wrap up tight in your eiderdown."

"Don't put my nightgown on?" Dorothy asked in disbelief, looking at Mam.

Mam shrugged. "I suppose the rules are different here."

Frank and Patrick poured water on the fire as Dorothy stepped into the tent. The embers sizzled while she rolled the eiderdown around herself. That same fluffy quilt brought the fancy cups all the way from England and only two of them had broken! She heard Dad stamping out the last sparks from the campfire. Then her eyes closed.

Dorothy's eyes snapped open and stared into the dark. A sound had awakened her. It wasn't Dad's snoring. After sharing close quarters on the ship, she was used to that. She heard the soft whistle of Mam's breathing, sleeping beside Dad. Lydia purred quietly on her other side.

The air was freezing. Dorothy pulled her tam down to her eyebrows. Suddenly sharp yelps pierced her ears. She lay rigid with terror. Mournful echoes responded from somewhere deep in the night.

Finally Dorothy found her voice. "Dad, Dad! What is that?"

"Uhh," Dad moaned sleepily, "What's the matter?"

The chorus had stopped as suddenly as it started. "I heard some frightful howling," she whispered.

"Probably coyotes. We're in the wilderness, remember?"

"What...what are coyotes, Dad?"

"They're wild dogs. They like to sing to each other at night. Go back to sleep."

Singing dogs? thought Dorothy. *This is a strange place. Well, they must be happy if they're singing.* She sighed with relief.

She squirmed, trying to get more comfortable. The straw mattress beneath her wasn't thick enough to smooth out the ground. Its cotton ticking was icy cold if she shifted even slightly to a different spot. She hugged her arms across her chest. How could this country be so warm in the daytime and so cold at night?

Next morning Dad was up first and had porridge bubbling on the tin camp stove. Dorothy felt better after hot oatmeal slid down her throat.

"Dodie, Mr. Thorpe was already here wondering where Rose lost her doll. She badgered him as soon as she woke up."

"I'll get it now, Dad. Don't fret, I'll find my way back." Dorothy grinned. "We're the only tent with a rocking chair outside."

She ran toward the wooden buildings. They were easy to see, jutting above the tents. She crossed the railway tracks and walked the length of the boardwalk without any sign of Rose's rag doll. Where could it be? Finally she noticed a dusty lump in the road.

"What's wrong, Dodie?" It was Victor, carrying a large bag of flour.

"Rose's doll." Dorothy held up a bedraggled princess with a torn skirt and no arms.

"Oh," said Victor sympathetically. "It looks like one of the dogs chewed it. Did you hear them last night, singing to the coyotes?" Victor examined the doll. "You could try washing it," he said hopefully.

"I don't think Rose would want a Cinderella with no arms."

"Well," said Victor with a wicked grin, "the prince wouldn't need a wedding ring." The thought of an arm-less Cinderella sent them both into spasms of giggles.

When she stopped laughing, Dorothy realized what she had to do. She said, "I have something else for Rose."

They walked through the tent town together. "Victor, why did your mother tell me you needed to settle down? I think you're perfect just as you are."

"Mum always preached at me about improving my

lot in life. She said I was too wild to grow up to be a gentleman." Victor stopped at his tent. "Now she only wants me to carry provisions and haul ice from the river."

Dorothy laughed. "I'd rather carry provisions and haul ice than act prissy like a proper lady." She held the doll up. "I'll probably get as dirty as Cinderella when I start working on the farm."

"Give me her mangled majesty," said Victor. "I'll get rid of... I mean, uh, give her a proper burial."

Dorothy handed the broken doll to Victor and skipped back to her own tent. Dad was chopping wood. Mam and Lydia weren't there.

"Dad!" she called "Where's my trunk?"

Dad pointed to a pile of luggage underneath a groundsheet. "I wasn't planning to open these trunks until we reach the colony."

Dorothy saw Rose running toward her, with her mum shuffling behind. "Dad, I have an emergency." She whispered in his ear and he nodded.

"Dodie! Did you find Cinderella?"

Dorothy knelt down and looked Rose in the eye. "Cinderella went away to marry the prince but I have a new friend for you."

Rose's eyes opened wide. "You do?"

Dorothy led Rose to the trunk Dad had just opened. She dug down and pulled out a parcel bundled in a wool blanket. "Your mummy is having a baby soon. Do you want your very own baby to look after?"

Rose nodded wide-eyed.

Dorothy unwrapped the parcel. A cry caught in her throat when she saw the exquisite doll Gram had given her two months ago. A doll for an older girl, Gram had said, not a little girl like Rose. But Rose needed the doll much more than she did.

"His name is George. You'll have to be very careful with him."

Mrs. Thorpe eased herself carefully into Mam's rocking chair.

Rose ran to her mother clutching the doll. "Cinderella went to live with the prince but Dodie gave me a baby doll named George."

Mrs. Thorpe reached out and patted Dorothy's hand. "When we were sitting in the train," she said, "your mother told me about your little brother who died."

Dorothy nodded.

"If this baby's a boy, I shall name him George. People will think I named him after Mr. Lloyd, but actually it will be in memory of your brother." Mrs. Thorpe massaged her belly. "I just saw the doctor. He thinks the baby will be born any day."

Dorothy stared at the massive bulge protruding where Mrs. Thorpe's lap should have been. She wanted to ask how the baby would get out of there but she was too shy. Then Mam and Lydia returned with provisions and Dorothy had to peel potatoes.

That night Dorothy was awakened again by a noise, but it wasn't a coyote's howl. It was a high-pitched scream. Dorothy shivered. Suddenly an amber light glowed in the darkness, lurching toward them. Through the canvas Dorothy saw the outline of a man kneeling at their door.

"Mrs. Bolton, Mrs. Bolton! My wife needs help."

"Mr. Thorpe?" Dorothy asked uncertainly.

"Dorothy, for the love of God, wake your mother. My wife is having the baby now." Mr. Thorpe sounded frantic, like he was choking back sobs. "I'm going back to her." The amber light wobbled away and disappeared.

Dorothy leapt out of her quilt, groping for her parents' blankets two feet away. "Mam, wake up! Mrs. Thorpe is having her baby!"

"What?" Mam answered groggily. "It's just the coyotes again. Get back in bed."

"It's really happening, Mam," Dorothy's teeth chattered. "Mr. Thorpe was just here." She shook Mam's shoulders.

Another sharp cry sliced through the blackness. Mam sat up abruptly, sending Dorothy rolling onto the cold rubber groundsheet.

"Willy, wake up! Go rouse the doctor."

Dorothy watched the black silhouettes of her parents lace their boots and pull on their overcoats. Her stomach twisted. Dad untied the tent flap and they stepped out. Dorothy's throat felt tight. She heard Dad refasten the door while Mam hurried away.

Tomorrow she would ask Mam to explain why Mrs. Thorpe was in pain and Mr. Thorpe was so frightened. Or she could ask Lydia right now.

Dorothy looked at Lydia lying quietly under her eiderdown. She hadn't stirred through all the commotion. Reluctantly she nudged her sister. Lydia was always such a bear when she was wakened from a sound sleep.

"Go away!" Lydia rolled herself tight in her quilt.

"Wake up. Mrs. Thorpe is having her baby."

Between the shrill cries, Dorothy heard Rose wailing. She couldn't wait for Lydia. She tugged on her boots. Wrapping her eiderdown around her, she untied the flap again and stepped out into the frigid night.

Dorothy ran to the next tent. She heard Mam giving directions. "Just keep pushing, dear. Be quiet, Rose. Your mum is fine and you'll have a baby brother or sister soon." Mam's even voice sounded so reassuring. "Jasper, bring the lantern closer."

"Mr. Thorpe," Dorothy yelled, "pass Rose to me. I have a blanket for her."

Rose was thrust out the door and she enveloped the sobbing child in her thick eiderdown. She felt the hard lump of the porcelain doll in Rose's arms.

"Shh, Rose, you don't want to wake dolly. I'm taking you to my tent to cuddle up with Lydia." Under the quilt, Rose stopped bawling.

Dorothy guided her towards the Bolton's tent, looking ghostly in the moonlight. Saskatoon, this village of tents, was different from everything she had left in England.

At the tent door she stopped. She looked up at the great black dome of sky, shimmering with millions of pinpricks of light.

Rose started sniffling again. "I'm cold, Dodie."

Opening the tent flap, she pulled Rose inside. Lying on her straw mattress, they snuggled close to Lydia's warm body. Wrapped in Dorothy's arms, Rose fell asleep.

Dorothy strained to hear the muffled voices in the next tent. She knew the doctor was there now. Finally she heard a different sound, a long quivering cry. She'd never heard that sound before but she knew what it was –

the newborn baby!

For a long time, Dorothy lay awake, thinking about her new life. Was it only three weeks ago she had said goodbye to Gram and her best friend, Ada? She had come so far, across the ocean, through miles of forests. She had already found new friends who shared her dream of farming on the vast Canadian prairie.

Never doubt that there's something here, Dad had said. Dorothy knew she had found it. A landscape full of wonders, people who needed her and a new world that she would help build.

Author's Note

Imagine growing up in England at the end of the Queen Victoria's reign. Most adults believe the motto, "Children should be seen but not heard." Your feelings are rarely considered and you are expected to obey authority without question. Girls' lives are even more restricted than boys', by strict standards for "proper lady-like behaviour."

In 1903 your life suddenly changes. You board a ship to Canada and almost all the adults become seasick for several days. Your parents are too ill to think about you. You have the run of the ship.

In 1982, an elderly woman told me this story, chuckling when she remembered how she had embraced her new-found freedom. Luckily I recorded her conversation on tape, never imagining I would write a book about her twenty-five years later.

I still marvel at the vivid episodes recounted by Dorothy Holtby Boan on her journey to the Barr Colony. The fictional Dorothy in this story is inspired by young Dorothy Holtby's grit and determination. I also draw on the memories and relationships of another spunky young traveller, Mary Pinder, described in her book Gully Farm.

Most of the incidents in my novel were reconstructed from archival records. Many settlers kept diaries, wrote letters and created memoirs which recorded close-up details of their epic journey. One diary that I found particularly helpful was written by Dorothy Holtby's older brother, Robert, who was nineteen at the time. In my story, the words that Frank writes are quoted directly from Robert Holtby's diary.

I also pored over old Eaton's catalogues to research clothing fashions and household items. I read books written at the turn of the century to get a feel for how English people actually spoke, especially working-class folk.

In the Western Development Museum in Moose Jaw, I sat in an old CPR colonist coach with simple wooden seats. At Heritage Village in Calgary, I received a personal tour through a tourist coach and learned how to pull the velour seats out to make beds, just as Dorothy does in the story.

Again, imagine living in Victorian England at the height of its power, with colonies around the world. An expression of the day is, "The sun never sets on the British Empire." In school you learn that you are a member of the most advanced civilization in the world. If your family has money and status or aspires to these things, you also grow up learning that you are superior to working-class people.

These beliefs, declared by actual Barr Colonists, are preserved in the archives for anyone to read. In this novel, some of my characters express these attitudes of superiority.

The letters and diaries also capture the colonists' sense of humour and the determination to make their dreams succeed. Unlike many immigrant groups, who fled persecution or famine, the British left relatively comfortable lives. They came seeking the opportunity to own land and to improve their social status.

In all, three thousand Britishers answered Isaac Barr's call to make the Canadian prairie more British. Although some returned home in disappointment, many worked hard to develop successful farms and businesses in the area around Lloydminster. Thousands of their descendants live across Canada today.

Glossary of Terms

Barr Colony: In 1902 the Reverend Isaac Montgomery Barr published letters in British newspapers inviting people to join a new settlement in the Canadian west. He promised comfortable transportation to this British-only colony, which would include a hospital, school and co-operative store to meet all the needs of the inhabitants. The colonists grew bitter toward Barr when these unrealistic promises were not kept.

bell tent: A cone-shaped canvas tent used by soldiers in the Boer War. Isaac Barr bought hundreds of used bell tents from the Canadian Government and sold them to colonists for $5.00 each.

Boer War: A war between Great Britain and South Africa (1899–1902). The Boers were South Africans of Dutch descent. Britain won the war and absorbed South Africa into the British Empire.

British Empire: Countries around the world controlled and governed by Britain, for economic or military advantage.

cab: A horse and carriage for hire.

carver's chair: A dining chair with arms, intended for the person who carves the meat.

colony: 1) A country that is ruled by another country. 2) A group of people who share a common culture and live apart from the rest of the population.

dear: 1) Expensive.
2) Much loved.

eiderdown: A quilt stuffed with the soft feathers from the eider duck (or other soft material); a duvet.

emigrate: Leave a country permanently to move to another country.

game: Wild animals or birds hunted for sport or food.

gamekeeper: A person employed by a landowner to protect game on his property.

hob: A flat metal shelf at the side of a fireplace, used for heating a pan.

immigrate: Move into a country permanently.

Manchester Guardian: An influential English newspaper, now known as *The Guardian*.

muffler: Scarf.

nowt: Nothing (rhymes with "out").

peaky: 1) Sickly.
2) White faced.

purser: The man who kept the ship's records and checked ticket sales against actual passengers to identify stowaways. On the Barr Colony voyage no stowaways were found.

rashers: Slices of bacon.

row: Argument (rhymes with "how").

scullery: A small room off the kitchen for washing dishes.

singlet: Undershirt.

smallpox: A deadly, contagious disease with high fever and skin eruptions. Throughout history the smallpox virus was responsible for many epidemics. In 1980 the World Health Organization announced that the disease had been wiped out by a worldwide vaccination program.

steamer trunk: A wooden travelling chest with a flat hinged lid, usually covered with canvas or leather.

tam o' shanter: A round knitted or cloth hat, originally from Scotland.

typhoid fever: A contagious disease with high fever, delirium and abdominal pain. Before antibiotics were developed, the symptoms lasted about a month, leaving the patient much weakened.

Dorothy's Journey
by Rail, 1903

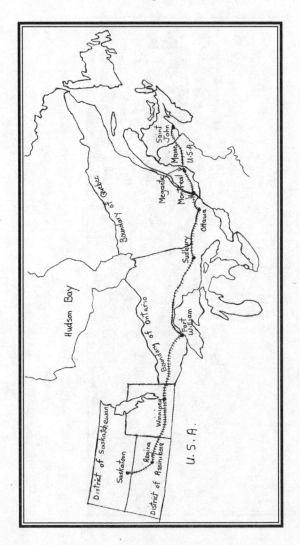

Author's hand drawn map showing the route from Saint John to Saskatoon.

The S.S. *Lake Manitoba* was built in 1901. This steamship made two trips to the Boer War as a cargo ship. Licensed for 750 passengers, she carried over 2000 Barr Colonists to Canada.

Photo courtesy of the Norway Heritage collection Source:www.heritage-ships.com

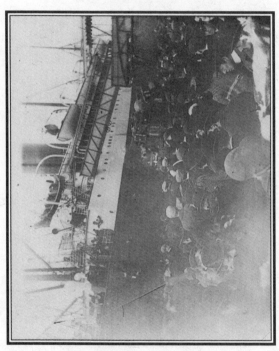

Photo courtesy of the Western Development Museum Collection, Saskatoon.

The S.S. *Lake Manitoba* is docked at Liverpool, England. Passengers crowd together on the landing stage waiting to board.

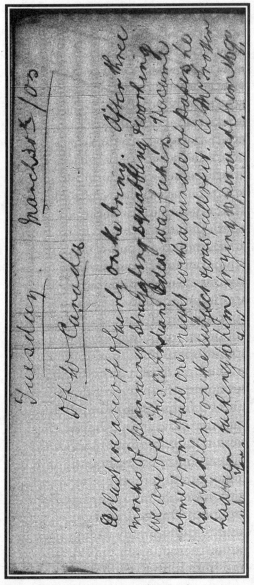

This is the first page of Robert Holtby's diary, written March 30th /03.

"At last we are off and fairly on the briny. After three months of planning, struggling, squabbling & working we are off. This Canadian idea was fathers. He came home from Hull one night with a bundle of papers he had had lent on the subject & was full of it. A Mr. Trotter had been talking to him trying to persuade him to go..."

Photo courtesy of the Western Development Museum Collection, Saskatoon.

Taken aboard ship, this photo shows the ship's captain on the left. The tall man next to him is the Reverend George Exton Lloyd. Notice his bowler hat and flowing black cape. The Reverend I.M. Barr is seated in front.

Photo courtesy of the Lloydminster and District Archives (#50)

A crowd of Barr Colonists disembark at a train station, possibly Winnipeg. There is one woman in the left corner; all the rest appear to be men. This is either the first or second train which carried unmarried people. The third and fourth trains carried families.

This photo shows the Barr Colony camp across the tracks from the village of Saskatoon. The colonists live here while they prepare to trek to their homesteads. The Canadian Government has just built a two-story immigration hall to welcome the colonists.

Photo courtesy of the Saskatoon Public Library, Local History Room (LH-2780)

Colonists inspect a shipment of Bain wagons, just unloaded from a C.P.R. freight train. These wagons have red wheels and a wooden box painted green. A canvas top with hoops and a spring-mounted seat can be purchased separately.

Photo courtesy of the Saskatoon Public Library, Local History Room (LH-2001)

Acknowledgements

Many thanks to my writing buddies, Alison Lohans and Sharon Hamilton, who experienced Dorothy's journey chapter by chapter as I wrote. Your feedback was invaluable in shaping this story. How lucky that we live in the same neighbourhood!

I am grateful to Lynne Bowen, author of *Muddling Through, The Remarkable Story of the Barr Colony*. Your extensive research and thorough crediting of sources made it much easier for me to find archival material. Thank you, also, for reading the manuscript and sharing a pleasant afternoon over coffee.

The details of my story came to life through the resources of the Saskatchewan Archives Board, the Barr Colony Museum, the Western Development Museums and the Prairie History Room at the Regina Public Library.

Thanks to friends Lorna Tyler, Judy Brindle and Wilfred Burton who critiqued the manuscript with fresh eyes. Three young readers, Jadyn Patton, Erin McLellan and Kaya Martin ensured that the text is kid-friendly. Dorian and Robert Smith walked me through the English money system, provided English expressions and shared memories of Yorkshire.

I want to thank my friend, Bregje Melissen, who introduced me to Dorothy Boan in 1982 and insisted that I tape her memories. Bregje continues to champion this story by introducing me to Dorothy's relatives and descendants.

A special thanks to my family who lived with this

narrative for a very long time. Kara and Jadyn graciously listened to several drafts. Sika helped me craft the structure of the story. My husband, Waldo, offered ongoing support and made the technology work, as always.

Finally, thank you to Barbara Sapergia at Coteau Books for believing in this story and making it happen.

About the Author

Anne Patton's popular books for children include *Fiddle Dancer* and *Dancing in My Bones* – books which explore Metis culture through the world of dance – and *Song Lei in a New Land*, about a Chinese girl who arrives in the Queen City [Regina] expecting to find a queen. Born in Ontario, Anne Patton taught elementary school in Regina for many years, before retirement launched her into her career as a prolific children's author.

In her spare time Anne enjoys camping, hiking and having adventures of all kinds.

ENVIRONMENTAL BENEFITS STATEMENT

Coteau Books saved the following resources by printing the pages of this book on chlorine free paper made with 100% post-consumer waste.

TREES	WATER	SOLID WASTE	GREENHOUSE GASES
15 FULLY GROWN	**10,043** GALLONS	**1,270** POUNDS	**3,300** POUNDS

 Calculation based on the methodological framework of Paper Calculator 2.0 - EDF